WITH A SIDE OF DEATH

THE EB EATS DINER MYSTERIES
BOOK 3

POPPY BRIDGEMAN

Ebook ISBN: 978-1-990509-76-6
Paperback ISBN: 978-1-990509-77-3

Cover created by Getcovers

FREE BOOK

Claim your copy of Burned by BLT when you sign up for my newsletter learn how Eliza became so determined to clear her name. Use the QR code below to get your free copy.

1

_____

The morning rush at EB Eats was in full swing, and I was exactly where I liked to be—coordinating from the dining room while Jacquie worked her magic in the kitchen. The familiar sounds of sizzling bacon and clinking coffee cups created the perfect soundtrack for a Monday morning in Nueva Vida.

"Order up!" Jacquie called, sliding a plate of her signature green chili scramble across the pass-through. "Table six, extra hot sauce on the side."

I grabbed the plate, inhaling the rich aroma that had made EB Eats a local favorite. Having Jacquie handle the cooking meant I could focus on what I did best—managing the front of house, talking to customers, and keeping an eye on the bigger picture of running the diner.

"Those kids are back," Lissa mentioned quietly, nodding toward the window as she refilled coffee cups.

I glanced across the street and spotted three teenagers doing a terrible job at trying to look casual. The Devil Dogs—Nueva Vida's wannabe gang that was more nuisance than real threat, but still a growing concern for parents in town.

"Those ones are harmless," Will said, appearing at my shoulder with a coffeepot. There was an edge to his voice though, the tension that always surfaced when the subject of his former associates came up. Will had managed to extract himself from that crowd, but it hadn't been easy. "Mostly just bored kids looking for something to belong to."

"Speaking of which," I said, "how is it going with your idea for a solution?"

Will nodded, his expression growing more serious. "Yeah, I've been talking to some people about a different approach. Community-based stuff instead of just punishment. But—"

The bell above the door chimed as George Kramer stumbled in, his usual neat appearance disheveled and his badge clipped to his belt. Detective George Kramer was not a man who did disheveled—rumpled, yes—which meant something significant had happened.

"Coffee," he said without preamble, sliding into the nearest booth. "Strong coffee. And whatever Jacquie's got ready back there."

I glanced over at Lissa, who was already reaching for the coffeepot. George had been a regular since I'd opened, and one of the men I was currently dating.

"Rough morning?" I asked, settling into the booth across from him.

"You could say that." He took a long gulp of coffee and seemed to steady himself. "Crime scene at Serenity Springs Retreat. Found a body about two hours ago."

My stomach dropped. Serenity Springs was just outside town—a small wellness retreat that catered to people looking for meditation, yoga, and organic food. The kind of peaceful place where the worst problem should be running out of herbal tea.

"Anyone we know?" I asked, dreading the answer.

"Linda Ramos."

The coffee cup slipped in my hands, and I had to set it down carefully to keep from spilling. I'd been here long enough to get to know the community, so I knew her. Linda Ramos taught third grade at the elementary school, organized the annual book fair, and volunteered at every community event. She was the person everyone liked—genuinely kind, never involved in town drama, always ready to help.

"That's impossible," I said. "Linda's... she's Linda. Nobody would want to hurt her."

"Poison," George said grimly. "In food that was prepared by a caterer who's now sitting in our holding cell."

Before I could process that fully, the front door exploded open with theatrical force that could only mean one person: Alistair McKay, owner of Dunes and my self-appointed nemesis.

"You!" he announced, sweeping into the diner like he was making an entrance at the opera and storming up to me. "You must help my cousin!"

George's shoulders sagged. "Please tell me you're not about to get involved in this."

"Involved?" Alistair pulled off his driving gloves with a flourish. "My dear Detective Kramer, I am already involved. The accused—this innocent caterer who has been so wrongfully imprisoned—is my cousin Derek!"

The diner had gone quiet, customers pausing mid-conversation to listen to what was going to be quite a performance.

"Your cousin Derek," I repeated, trying to separate the drama from the real information.

"Derek Hartwell, finest caterer in the Southwest,

wouldn't poison a mosquito, much less a beloved school teacher!" Alistair gestured dramatically. "He called me from jail not twenty minutes ago, completely devastated. This is clearly a case of being in the wrong place at the wrong time."

George rubbed his temples. "Alistair, this is an active investigation—"

"Which is precisely why Eliza must get involved immediately!" Alistair turned to me with the intensity of someone presenting life-or-death information. "You solved those other murders. Derek needs your expertise."

"Other murders?" one tourist whispered to her husband.

"I'm not a detective," I said firmly, though my mind was already spinning. Linda Ramos was dead, and someone had been arrested. Someone who was innocent, if Alistair was to be believed—which wasn't a given.

"But you are brilliant at solving crimes," Alistair insisted. "Derek prepared breakfast for the retreat participants yesterday morning, then left at eight-thirty. He was catering a lunch event across town from noon to four—dozens of witnesses. But Linda died sometime in the afternoon from poison that was allegedly in food he prepared hours earlier."

George's expression sharpened. "How do you know the timeline?"

"Derek told me everything during our phone call. He's being completely cooperative, but he's terrified. A small-business owner like him, even if charges are dropped, the reputation damage could destroy everything he's built."

I looked at George, whose exhaustion was even more apparent now. "This just happened this morning?"

"Body was discovered at seven AM by the retreat coordinator," he confirmed. "Derek was arrested at his apartment an hour later. We haven't charged him yet."

"And you're sure it was poison?" I'd been the focus of too many accusations of food-related deaths—none of them my doing.

George shrugged wearily. "I guess in this town the gossip mill will be spinning out facts and fiction equally. So, I don't talk about ongoing investigations, but yes, it looks like poison."

I felt that familiar tug, the same one that had gotten me into trouble before—and solved two murders in the process. Linda Ramos was dead, and if Derek was innocent, then someone else had killed a woman everyone loved. Someone who was still free. And George would be bound by rules making it hard to get to the truth fast.

"What kind of poison?" I asked.

George hesitated, then seemed to decide I'd find out, anyway. "Too early to know for certain, but possibly something in her afternoon snack. Energy bars that Derek prepared that morning."

"Energy bars?" Alistair looked angry. "But Derek makes the most magnificent energy bars—all organic ingredients, locally sourced when possible. They're works of art!"

"Which is probably why Linda ate one," George said. "According to the retreat coordinator, Linda always had one of Derek's energy bars at exactly three PM as part of her meditation routine."

The implications hit me immediately. If the killer knew Linda's routine—knew she'd eat one of those bars at a specific time—then this wasn't random. This was planned.

"George," I said carefully, "if Derek left at eight-thirty in the morning, how would he know Linda would eat a specific energy bar? Wouldn't they all be sitting out for anyone to take?"

"That's... actually a good question." George looked at me with the mixed expression he got when he realized I was already thinking like an investigator. He didn't like my getting into dangerous situations, but he knew I had skills. "One we'll be looking into."

"See!" Alistair clapped his hands together. "She's already identified the crucial flaw in your case. Derek couldn't have targeted Linda specifically unless—" He stopped, his dramatic expression faltering. "Unless he knew her routine. Which he did, because he'd been catering there for three days."

The temporary excitement on his face crumpled into worry.

"Which brings us back to motive," George said. "Why would your cousin want Linda Ramos dead?"

"He wouldn't! Derek's never met a person he didn't like. He baked her birthday cake last year." Alistair turned to me, with desperation replacing drama. "Eliza, you have to help. Derek didn't do this, so someone else did. Someone who wanted Linda dead and was clever enough to frame an innocent caterer."

I looked around the diner. Will was listening intently while pretending to wipe down tables. Jacquie had appeared in the kitchen doorway, concern evident on her face. Even the tourists were hanging on every word.

"George," I said, "what can you tell us about the retreat? Who else was there?"

"I said I can't discuss details of an active investigation." But his tone suggested he wasn't entirely opposed to the idea of unofficial help. "However, I can say that there were several other participants, and we'll be interviewing all of them."

"Of course you will," I said. "And I'm sure they'll be forthcoming with the police about anything unusual they might have noticed."

George gave me a look that said he hadn't missed my sarcasm. Small-town people might clam up around official investigators, but they'd talk to someone they trusted—someone who owned the local diner and had a reputation for helping people.

"I suppose," he said, "if someone were to, say, visit the retreat in a completely unofficial capacity—maybe to offer condolences or see if anyone needed support during this difficult time—that would be understandable community care."

Alistair beamed. "Brilliant! Eliza, we should go immediately—"

"We?" I raised an eyebrow.

"You'll need someone who knows Derek's work, who can speak to his character and methods. Plus, I have extensive experience in matters of investigation."

I looked at George, who was studying his coffee cup with great interest. "If I were to visit the retreat—purely to offer community support, of course—would that interfere with your investigation?"

"As long as any concerned citizen stayed out of the way of official police work and shared any relevant information they might learn..." He shrugged. "I can't stop people from caring about their neighbors."

Jacquie appeared at the table with a plate of her breakfast special—eggs over easy, thick-cut bacon, and hash browns that were crispy on the outside and fluffy inside. "On the house," she told George. "You look like you need it."

"Thanks, Jacquie. You're a lifesaver."

I watched him dig into the food with obvious relief our discussion was over. I made my decision and didn't give him the opportunity to argue. Linda Ramos deserved justice, Derek deserved a fair investigation, and Nueva Vida deserved to know the truth.

"Alistair," I said, "leave this to me, Kashvi and Jet."

He glared at me as if I'd told him to leave it to the cops. "He's my cousin."

"And your approach is to yell, blame, and bully." I couldn't have him scaring people off.

Alistair didn't have a subtle side. I could see his determination and hope for Derek's release battling across his face. After a moment when I didn't back down, he said, "I agree to let you try to do this without me. But I will not sit back and let you destroy Derek's life." He marched to the door and flung it open.

2

After the lunch rush died down and Jacquie had the kitchen well in hand, I drove home with more questions than answers swirling through my mind. Linda Ramos was dead, Derek McKay was in jail, and Alistair was convinced his cousin was innocent. The logical next step was what we'd done twice before: gather the people I trusted most and try to make sense of the impossible.

Macchiato greeted me at the front door with her usual judgmental expression, as if my absence had personally inconvenienced her. Her long black fur was perfectly groomed, the white blaze making her look like a furry magistrate ready to hear my explanation.

"Don't give me that look," I told her, scratching behind her ears. "We might have another case, and you know how these things go."

She purred, then stalked toward her food bowl to remind me of my domestic duties.

My phone buzzed with a reply to the group I'd sent before I left the diner calling for a meeting at my place.

Kashvi responded immediately: *A new case? I heard some rumors?*

Looks like it.

Jet's reply was more practical: *Should I bring snacks?*

I've got it covered.

By two o'clock, my living room had transformed into our unofficial investigation headquarters. Kashvi sat cross-legged on the floor with her laptop open and her purple hair catching the afternoon sunlight streaming through the windows. Jet had claimed the comfortable chair by the bookshelf, his long legs stretched out and a notepad balanced on his knee. Macchiato had positioned herself on the coffee table like a fuzzy supervisor, yellow eyes tracking our movements.

"Okay," I said, settling onto the couch with my notebook. "Here's what we know. Linda Ramos was found dead this morning at Serenity Springs Retreat. Poison, probably in food prepared by Derek Hartwell, who is Alistair's cousin and who is currently sitting in jail."

"Wait," Kashvi said, fingers pausing over her keyboard. "Linda Ramos? The elementary school teacher? She volunteers at the literacy center every week."

"That's the one." I flipped open my notebook to the notes I'd made during the morning's chaos. "According to George, she died sometime yesterday afternoon from poison that was allegedly in energy bar Derek had prepared that morning."

Jet frowned. "That seems like a pretty big window for something to go wrong. If Derek made the food in the morning and Linda died in the afternoon, anyone could have tampered with it."

"Exactly what I was thinking." I looked at my notes again. "Derek left the retreat at eight-thirty had an alibi for the afternoon. He was catering an event across town with dozens of witnesses."

Kashvi was typing everything into a document. "So either Derek somehow managed to poison Linda's food in a way that would affect her hours later, or someone else did it after he left."

"And if someone else did do it," Jet said, "they had to know Linda would eat that specific energy bar. That suggests planning, not opportunity."

My phone rang, interrupting the analysis. Alistair's name flashed on the screen, and I put it on speaker even though every instinct told me to ignore it.

"Eliza! Thank goodness you answered. I've just spoken with Derek again, and there are details—crucial details— that I must share immediately!"

"We're listening, Alistair."

"First, the retreat coordinator is a woman named Serenity Walsh—yes, that's her real name—who runs the place like a military operation. Very specific schedules, very particular about who does what and when."

Kashvi added the information.

"What else?" I asked to keep him on topic.

"Derek specifically mentioned that Linda seemed nervous yesterday morning. She kept asking about the other participants' schedules, like she was avoiding someone or watching for someone."

Kashvi looked up from her laptop. "That's interesting. Did Derek say who else was at the retreat?"

"Several people! There's Dr. Zhang—some kind of medical professional from Phoenix—and Emily Stone-house, you know her, owns the tourist trap on Main Street. Plus a few others Derek didn't know well."

"Emily was there?" I asked, surprised. Emily's boutique

specialized in tourist souvenirs, and she always had a side gig in sales—not exactly the granola-and-meditation crowd I'd expect at Serenity Springs.

"Oh yes, and Derek said Linda was particularly interested in talking to Emily and Dr. Zhang. She kept asking them questions that went beyond normal getting-to-know-you kind of conversation."

Jet leaned forward as if he had to get closer to interrupt Alistair. "What kind of questions?"

"Derek wasn't close enough to hear specifics. And good caterers stay out of gossip! He told me Emily looked uncomfortable and Dr. Zhang seemed annoyed. Linda was being... persistent."

I exchanged glances with Kashvi. Linda Ramos had always struck me as genuinely nice, the teacher we all remember who knew every student's name and never said an unkind word about anyone. The idea of her making people uncomfortable was strange.

"There's something else," Alistair continued, his voice dropping to a conspiratorial whisper. "Derek mentioned that Linda always had one of his energy bars at exactly three PM as part of her meditation routine. Same time every day for all three days she'd been there."

"So anyone who knew her routine could predict when she'd eat the bar," I said. Not news but good to have confirmation of any facts.

"Precisely! Which means the killer had to be someone who'd observed her patterns. Someone at the retreat. This should be simple! You need to get out there right away!"

Macchiato chose that moment to stand up and stretch, her claws clicking against the coffee table surface. She swatted at an imaginary fly.

"Alistair," I said, "we need to talk to Derek directly. Can you arrange that?"

"Absolutely! He's been released on bail—my lawyer worked absolute miracles. Derek's staying at my house until this is resolved. Could you come by this evening? Say, seven o'clock?"

The last place I wanted to be was stuck in Alistair's home, but maybe Derek was on house arrest. "We'll be there."

After hanging up, I looked at my team. Printed articles about Serenity Springs Retreat surrounded Kashvi. All data for our murder board later if we had time. Jet was making a timeline on a fresh page of his notepad. And Macchiato was staring at me, but whether she needed food, water, cuddles, or a lap, I couldn't tell.

"So," Kashvi said, "we have a beloved school teacher who was acting strangely, asking invasive questions at a wellness retreat. She's killed by poison in food prepared by an innocent caterer, but the timing suggests someone else had access to the food after he left."

"And the killer had to know Linda's exact routine to target her," Jet added.

I stood up and walked to the window, looking out at the desert landscape that had become home. Somewhere out there, a killer was walking free while Derek sat in Alistair's house, probably terrified that his life was falling apart. We seemed to be going over the same few details, but that's all we had right now.

I turned back to my friends. "why would anyone want Linda Ramos dead?"

"Maybe she wasn't as beloved as everyone thought," Kashvi suggested quietly. "You know, the guy who goes on a killing spree and neighbors all say he was a nice quite guy?"

"That would mean the entire town was fooled," Jet said, "I can't believe that's the case."

My phone buzzed with a text from Will: *Tribal council meeting this afternoon went great. They're really interested in the restorative justice approach. Mayor Hendricks is backing the program 100%.*

I showed the text to the others. "At least something good is happening today."

"The mayor is pretty progressive," Kashvi asked.

I thought about the few times I'd met her—always professional, always seemed invested in making Nueva Vida better. "Will's been working on this gang intervention idea with the tribal council. Alternative to just arresting kids."

"Good for him," Jet said. "Nice to have local officials who care about actually solving problems."

I looked at the notes spread across my coffee table, at my friends ready to help solve another impossible case, at Macchiato supervising with feline authority. When I moved to Nueva Vida to open my diner, I didn't know I'd be getting into the murder-solving game.

"Okay," I said, settling back on the couch. "Let's plan our approach. We need to visit the retreat, but we also need to be careful. If Linda was killed for asking too many questions, we don't want to paint targets on our own backs."

"Agreed," Kashvi said. "How about we start by offering condolences to the retreat coordinator? Show community support during a difficult time?"

"Perfect cover," Jet nodded. "We're concerned neighbors, not investigators."

"And we listen more than we talk," I added. "Let people tell us what they think happened."

Macchiato jumped down from the coffee table and

stalked toward her favorite sunny spot by the sliding glass door, her tail twitching with what I interpreted as approval.

"Meeting tonight at seven with Derek and Alistair," I said, checking my watch. "Tomorrow morning we visit Serenity Springs Retreat. And we figure out who wanted Linda Ramos dead and why."

3

D erek's account of the situation was the same as Alistair's, without the drama and hyperbole. Even though we left with no new clues, it was important that we hear his firsthand account. So the next morning, I headed toward Serenity Springs Retreat with Kashvi riding shotgun and a thermos of Jacquie's coffee between us. The desert air was crisp and clear, the kind of morning that made me grateful to live in New Mexico. Today, though, I needed to focus on the questions that had kept me awake half the night.

"Remember," I said as we pulled into the gravel parking lot, "we're here to offer community support and condolences. We're not investigating anything."

"Right," Kashvi said. She patted her messenger bag that held her notebook and the research she'd printed about the retreat. "Just concerned neighbors."

Serenity Springs Retreat looked exactly like what it was —a place designed to help people disconnect from the world and reconnect with themselves. Low adobe buildings scattered around a central courtyard, with carefully tended desert gardens and strategically placed benches for contemplation. Under different circumstances, it would have seemed peaceful. Today, it felt like a crime scene trying to pretend everything was normal.

Serenity Walsh met us at the main building's entrance, and I could see why she'd chosen her name. Tall and willowy, with long blond hair and flowing earth-toned clothing, she moved with the deliberate grace from years of yoga practice. Her voice was soft and measured, the tone that probably worked wonders for stressed-out retreat participants.

"Eliza, I'm so glad you came," she said, clasping my hands in both of hers. "This has been such a difficult time for all of us."

"I can only imagine," I said, allowing her to lead us into a large common room decorated with crystals, plants, and inspirational quotes painted on the walls in elegant script. "How are your other participants holding up?"

"Everyone's struggling, of course," Serenity said, gesturing for us to sit on cushioned benches arranged around a low table. "Most our our out of town visitors have found other accommodation, only a few locals are still here. Linda was such a bright presence here. She had this natural warmth that made everyone feel welcome."

Kashvi and I exchanged subtle glances. That wasn't exactly how Derek had described Linda's interactions with the other participants, but pressing the point immediately would be too obvious.

"Had Linda been to the retreat before?" I asked.

"This was her first time, but she'd been asking about our programs for months. Said she was dealing with some difficult decisions and needed clarity." Serenity's hands fluttered nervously, despite her calm tone. "She seemed particularly interested in our meditation practices and community-building exercises."

"Community-building?" Kashvi asked casually.

"We encourage participants to share their stories, to support each other through whatever challenges brought them here." Serenity's smile looked slightly forced. "Linda was very... engaged in that process. Perhaps more so than some people were comfortable with."

There it was—the first crack in the perfectly serene facade.

"What do you mean by that?" I asked gently.

Serenity was quiet for a moment, staring out the large windows at the desert landscape. "Linda had this instinct to want to help everyone. But sometimes people come here specifically to avoid talking about their problems, and she could be quite persistent in her attempts to connect. Some attendees want to meditate rather than consult."

Before I could follow up on that interesting statement, voices from the courtyard caught my attention. Through the windows, I could see two people in what looked like an intense conversation near one of the meditation gardens—a middle-aged man with graying hair gesturing emphatically while talking to a younger woman I recognized who kept shaking her head.

"Are those other retreat participants?" I asked.

"Yes," Serenity said, her serene mask slipping another notch. "Dr. James Zhang and Emily Stonehouse. They're both... processing Linda's death in their own ways."

I knew Emily—she owned Stonehouse Boutique on Main Street and was always involved in some new business venture, maybe not shady, but not exactly straight either. Dr. Zhang was unfamiliar, but the way Serenity said his name suggested there was more to his story.

"They look upset," Kashvi observed.

"Everyone's been on edge since yesterday," Serenity admitted. "The police questioned everyone extensively, and some people are taking it harder than others."

"Would it be possible to speak with them?" I asked. "Just to offer our support as community members?"

Serenity hesitated, clearly torn between her role as gracious hostess and her obvious desire to protect her remaining participants from further stress.

"I suppose that would be all right," she said finally. "But please be sensitive. Everyone's grieving and traumatized."

We made our way to the courtyard, where the desert air carried the scent of sage and blooming desert willow. Dr. Zhang and Emily had moved apart but were still standing near the meditation garden, both looking distinctly uncomfortable.

"Emily," I called, approaching with what I hoped was an appropriately sympathetic expression.

She turned, and I could see the stress lines around her eyes. Her usually perfect makeup was minimal, and her clothing—while still stylish—looked like it had been chosen for comfort rather than impression.

"Oh, Eliza and Kashvi," she said, relief evident in her voice. "I didn't expect to see anyone from town."

"We came to check on everyone," I said, including Dr. Zhang in my greeting nod. "This must be so difficult."

Dr. Zhang, who had been standing quietly during our exchange, stepped forward. He was probably in his late fifties, with intelligent eyes behind wire-rimmed glasses and the posture that came from years of leaning forward to listen to his patients.

"Dr. James Zhang," he said, extending his hand. "I don't believe we've met."

"Eliza Burton. I own EB Eats in town."

"The diner with the excellent coffee," he said with a weak smile. "Linda mentioned it several times. She said you made the best green chili breakfast burritos in New Mexico."

"I'm Kashvi, bookstore owner. Good to meet you too." She held out her hand for him to shake.

"Ah, I don't read much, but I've seen your store," Dr. Zhang said.

"Linda was always supportive of local businesses," I said. "She'll be missed by the whole community."

"She was... very interested in everyone here," Emily said carefully, glancing at Dr. Zhang. "Always asking questions, wanting to know about people's lives."

"That sounds like Linda," Kashvi said. "She had that strong curiosity about people."

Dr. Zhang's expression grew guarded. "Some of us come to retreats specifically to get away from questions and expectations. Linda seemed to struggle with respecting those boundaries."

There was an edge to his voice that suggested Linda's questions had been more than casually intrusive.

Kashvi tensed at my side, like she thought I needed a prompt to follow the topic. "What kinds of questions was she asking?" I asked, trying to sound merely curious rather than investigative.

Emily and Dr. Zhang exchanged a look that seemed to contain an entire conversation.

"Personal things," Emily said finally. "About our backgrounds, our reasons for being here, financial situations. She said she was working on some kind of community documentation project, but it felt..."

"Invasive," Dr. Zhang finished. "I'm sure she meant well,

but some of us have come here to escape scrutiny, not invite more of it."

"That sounds awful," Kashvi said. "Coming here to find some peace and then being poked and prodded for information."

"Perhaps not that aggressive," Dr. Zhang said. "Just too eager to step into my personal space."

Serenity had followed us to the courtyard and was hovering nearby, clearly uncomfortable with the direction of the conversation.

"Linda was just trying to connect with people," she said, her voice carrying a note of defensiveness. "She had this natural warmth that made her want to help everyone."

"Warmth can become intrusive when people don't want to be helped," Dr. Zhang said with a touch of exasperation.

The tension in the group was palpable, and I realized we'd stumbled into something more complex than simple grief over a beloved community member's death. I couldn't wait to get Kashvi's take on the dynamic.

My phone buzzed with a text, Lissa: *Are you coming in? Lunch rush is hitting hard.*

"I'm sorry," I said, "but we need to get back to town. Thank you for talking with us. If there's anything the community can do to support you during this difficult time..."

"Actually," Emily said quickly, "would it be possible to continue this conversation somewhere else? I mean, if you're trying to understand what happened to Linda, I think there are things you should know."

Dr. Zhang nodded reluctantly. "Perhaps we could meet at your diner later today? Away from..." He gestured vaguely at the retreat buildings.

"Of course," I said. "How about this afternoon? Two o'clock?"

After exchanging contact information, Kashvi and I made our way back to the car, both of us processing what we'd just learned.

"So Linda wasn't just asking friendly getting-to-know-you questions," Kashvi said as we drove back toward town.

"Definitely not. And both Emily and Dr. Zhang seem genuinely uncomfortable about whatever she was asking."

"I wonder whether they're uncomfortable because Linda was being pushy, or because she was getting close to something they didn't want exposed."

4

By two o'clock, EB Eats had settled into its comfortable afternoon rhythm. The lunch rush had cleared out, leaving behind the lingering scent of Jacquie's famous bacon cheeseburgers. The only people around were the few coffee drinkers, and one woman who stared at her laptop as if she could force it to work. I'd changed the coffee to a fresh pot of our afternoon blend—a little lighter than the morning's strong brew—and straightened the dining room while Jacquie hummed contentedly in the kitchen.

"Your company is here," Lissa called from the front window, where she was wiping down tables.

Through the glass, I could see Emily and Dr. Zhang approaching the diner, both looking more relaxed than they had at the retreat that morning. Emily had changed into leggings and an oversized shirt. Dr. Zhang wore khakis and a polo shirt, the casual attire suggesting he was headed for the golf course.

"I'll take the back booth," I told Lissa, grabbing three coffee cups and the thermal carafe. The booth in the far corner was our unofficial conference room—far enough from other customers to allow for private conversation, but still very much part of the diner's welcoming atmosphere.

"Eliza," Emily said as they settled into the cushioned seats, "thank you so much for this. I know it's an imposition."

"Not at all," I said, pouring coffee all around. "Can I get you anything to eat? Jacquie made chocolate chip cookies this morning, and I have to say they're dangerous."

Dr. Zhang's smile was the first relaxed expression I'd seen from him. "That sounds perfect. I haven't had a home-made chocolate chip cookie in months."

"Coming right up." I caught Jacquie's eye and pointed to the dessert display. She nodded and started arranging treats on one of our cheerful ceramic plates—the blue ones with tiny desert flowers that always made everything look more homey.

When I returned with the cookies, both Emily and Dr. Zhang looked like they'd decompressed from the morning's tension. There was something about EB Eats that did that to people—the warm lighting, the comfortable booths, the way the soft clatter from the kitchen created a cocoon of normalcy no matter what was going on outside.

"So," I said, settling into the booth across from them, "you mentioned you wanted to talk about Linda away from the retreat."

Emily and Dr. Zhang exchanged a look—not the guarded, nervous glance from the morning, but something more like shared resignation.

"Linda was asking very specific questions about our backgrounds," Emily said, breaking a cookie in half and examining it while she gathered her thoughts. "And I mean specific. Things she knew too much about."

"What kinds of details?" I asked, pulling out my small notebook—the one I kept for grocery lists and random thoughts, nothing that would make this feel like an official interrogation.

"She knew about my tax troubles," Emily said, her voice dropping to that careful tone people used when discussing things they'd rather forget. "I know it was pretty general knowledge, but she already knew more: the IRS penalty, the payment plan, even the specific amount I still owed. She asked if I was current on my payments and whether I was worried about another audit."

Dr. Zhang nodded grimly. "She somehow knew I'd left my practice in Phoenix under... complicated circumstances. Asked me directly about a malpractice inquiry that never became public."

I made notes, trying to process what they were telling me. "Did either of you tell her these things?"

"Absolutely not," Emily said firmly. "I barely know Linda beyond saying hello at community events. And those tax issues—I've worked very hard to put that mess behind me."

"Same here," Dr. Zhang said. "The situation in Phoenix was resolved, but it's not something I discuss with people I've just met."

Jacquie appeared at the table with the coffee pot, topping off everyone's cups without asking. "Everything okay over here?" she asked, her voice carrying just enough warmth to let them know she was available if needed, but not prying.

"Perfect, thank you," Dr. Zhang said, and I could see him relax even further. "These cookies are incredible."

"Family recipe," Jacquie said with pride. "I'll tell you the secret ingredient if you promise not to open a competing diner."

"I think I'll stick to medicine," he laughed, and for a moment the tension in the booth lifted completely.

After Jacquie returned to the kitchen, I leaned forward. "So Linda somehow had detailed information about both of your personal situations. Did she say how she knew?"

"That's the really strange part," Emily said, stirring sugar into her coffee with slow, thoughtful movements. "She said she was working on a community documentation project. Something about preserving Nueva Vida's history and the stories of people who'd made the town their home."

"But her questions didn't feel like historical documentation," Dr. Zhang added. "They felt more like... investigative journalism. Or detective work."

The bell over the front door chimed, and I looked up to see Kashvi entering with her laptop bag slung over her shoulder and her purple hair catching the afternoon light. She spotted us in the back booth and gave a small wave.

"Mind if I join you?" she asked.

"Please," I said, scooting over to make room. "Emily and Dr. Zhang were just telling me about Linda's questions at the retreat."

Kashvi settled in beside me, and I noticed how her presence seemed to make the conversation feel even more like a friendly gathering rather than an interrogation. She had that effect on people—a natural warmth that made strangers feel comfortable sharing things they might otherwise keep private.

"Were there other participants at the retreat who seemed uncomfortable with Linda's questions?" Kashvi asked, pulling out her own small notebook.

"Everyone, I think," Emily said. "Linda had this way of remembering everything you said and then asking follow-up questions later that revealed she'd been thinking about your answers. It was... unsettling."

Dr. Zhang nodded. "She asked me about my current living situation, whether I was planning to stay in Nueva Vida long-term, what had drawn me to the area. Normal questions, except she also somehow knew I'd been looking at rental properties before I bought my current place."

"How could she have known that?" I asked.

"That's what I'd like to know. Unless she was talking to real estate agents or..." He trailed off, looking uncomfortable.

"Or what?"

"Or she had some other way of accessing information about people's private business."

The implications of that hung in the air while we all sipped our coffee and contemplated what Linda might have been up to.

"Did anyone else at the retreat seem particularly bothered by her questions?" Kashvi asked.

Emily and Dr. Zhang looked at each other again, and this time I could see them having one of those silent conversations that happened between people who'd shared an unsettling experience.

"The other attendees were from out of town," Dr. Zhang said. "So she didn't interact with them much beyond a friendly hello."

"There was some tension between Linda and Serenity toward the end," Emily said finally. "Nothing dramatic, but Serenity seemed frustrated with how much time Linda was spending on personal conversations instead of participating in the retreat activities."

"And there was that argument on Sunday night," Dr. Zhang added reluctantly.

"What argument?" I asked.

"Linda and Serenity were talking in the courtyard after dinner. We couldn't hear what they were saying, but it definitely wasn't a friendly conversation. Serenity looked upset, and Linda seemed... determined about something."

I made more notes, my mind racing. Linda had been systematically gathering information about people's private business, had gotten into an argument with the retreat coordinator, and had been killed the next day. It looked like someone had wanted to stop her from whatever she was investigating.

"One more question," I said. "Did either of you get the impression that Linda was afraid of anything? Or anyone?"

"Not afraid, exactly," Emily said, considering. "But she was definitely observing people. Like she was waiting for something, or looking for some kind of confirmation about something she suspected."

"I think Linda had a theory she was trying to prove," Dr. Zhang agreed. "Whatever she was working on, she was very focused on it."

After they left, promising to call if they remembered anything else, Kashvi and I sat in the booth nursing our coffee and trying to make sense of what we'd learned.

"So Linda was investigating something," Kashvi said. "Something that involved digging into people's private information."

"And someone killed her to stop her from finding it, or from sharing what she'd already found."

"Which means," Kashvi said, "we need to figure out what Linda was really looking for."

5

M ayor Patricia Hendricks walked through the front door that evening, bringing with her a sense of purposeful energy that seemed to surround successful politicians. Even at the end of what was a long day, her silver hair was perfectly styled and her navy blazer looked crisp and professional.

"Mayor Hendricks," I called from behind the counter, where I was restocking the napkin dispensers while Jacquie finished cleaning the prep station. "This is a nice surprise."

"I hope you don't mind me dropping by without calling first," she said, settling onto one of the counter stools with an easy manner. I wondered if she was genuinely comfortable talking to constituents, or if the move was choreographed to make me feel included—it was hard to tell with politicians. "I wanted to catch you while things were quiet."

I poured her a cup of coffee and set it in front of her with cream and sugar. "Not at all. Can I get you something to eat? We still have some of the special available, chorizo hash with chili cornbread."

"That sounds wonderful," she said, warming her hands

around the coffee cup. "But actually, I wanted to talk to you about Will's proposal for addressing our gang situation. I've been following the developments closely, and I'm very impressed."

At the mention of Will's name, I glanced toward the dining room where he was clearing tables from the dinner service. He looked up, caught sight of the mayor, and nodded respectfully before continuing his work with perhaps a bit more attention to detail than usual.

"He's put a lot of thought into it," I said, ladling a generous portion of the hash into her bowl. "The whole restorative justice approach seems like it could make a difference for these kids."

"That's exactly what I think," Mayor Hendricks said, accepting the steaming bowl with obvious appreciation. "I've been in discussions with the tribal council leadership, and they're enthusiastic about partnering with the city on this. Mrs. Dosela speaks very highly of Will's understanding of both the problems and the potential solutions."

She took a bite of the hash with a chunk of cornbread and closed her eyes in appreciation. "Oh my goodness. This is incredible."

"Jacquie's secret ingredient," I said with a smile. "She guards that recipe like state secrets."

"Smart woman," the mayor laughed, then grew more serious. "The reason I wanted to talk to you is that not everyone is as enthusiastic about Will's approach as I am. Some people think we should take a harder line with these kids—arrest them, prosecute them, teach them a lesson through traditional consequences."

I could guess who she meant. Alistair had been vocal about his belief that "coddling juvenile delinquents" would only encourage more unacceptable behavior, and several longtime residents had expressed similar views at community meetings. I just hoped Detective Collett wasn't encouraging opposition to the plan.

"What's your position?" I asked, refilling her coffee cup.

"I believe in second chances," she said simply. "Not everyone gets the same opportunities in life, and sometimes kids make poor choices because they don't see better options. If we can show them there's another path—one that leads to being productive members of the community rather than adversaries of it—then that's worth trying."

There was something in her tone that suggested this wasn't just political rhetoric, but a genuine belief born from experience. I warmed to her even more than I had during our previous brief encounters at community events.

"Will mentioned that Detective Collett has concerns about the approach," I said carefully.

Mayor Hendricks nodded, stirring cream into her fresh coffee with thoughtful movements. "Detective Collett is worried that without serious consequences, the kids won't take the program seriously. She's concerned about setting precedents that might encourage other young people to think they can get away with criminal behavior."

"Those are legitimate concerns," I said.

"They are," she agreed. "And they're the kinds of concerns that come from someone who's seen the worst that people can do to each other. Law enforcement officers develop a certain perspective about human nature—they have to, in order to do their jobs effectively. But sometimes that perspective can limit their ability to see potential for change."

She took another bite of the hash and then continued. "I spent some time working in juvenile services early in my career, before I got into municipal government. I saw what happens when we treat kids like criminals instead of like community members who've lost their way. The recidivism rates are terrible, the costs are enormous, and the human toll is heartbreaking."

"What changed your mind about trying something different?"

"A fifteen-year-old named Evan," she said, her voice softening. "He'd been arrested three times for various minor offenses —vandalism, shoplifting, getting into fights. Everyone said he was headed for serious trouble, that jail time was the only thing that would get his attention. But his grandmother convinced a judge to try a community service program instead."

She smiled at the memory. "Evan spent six months working with a local nonprofit that helped elderly residents with home maintenance. He discovered he was good with his hands, good at solving practical problems. More importantly, he discovered that people valued his contributions. That grandmother was onto something—Evan didn't need to be punished, he needed to be useful."

"What happened to him?"

"He's a licensed contractor now, runs his own business, employs four people." Mayor Hendricks' smile widened. "He also volunteers with the same nonprofit program that helped him, mentoring other kids who've gotten into trouble."

I could see why Will's proposal had appealed to her so strongly. The parallels between Evan's story and what the tribal council was offering were obvious.

"So you're willing to back the program even though some people think it's too soft?" I asked.

"I'm willing to back it because I think it's smart," she said. "Punishment for its own sake doesn't solve problems—

it just satisfies people's desire for revenge. If we want to actually reduce crime and help young people become productive citizens, we need to focus on what works, not what makes us feel better about being tough on crime."

Will had finished his table-clearing duties and was approaching the counter, clearly wanting to join the conversation but uncertain about interrupting a discussion between his boss and the mayor.

"Will," I called, "come tell Mayor Hendricks about your meeting with Mrs. Dosela yesterday."

He brightened and moved closer, though he maintained the respectful posture that seemed to come naturally to him when talking to authority figures.

"It went really well," he said, addressing the mayor. "Mrs. Dosela explained how the traditional conflict resolution process works within the tribal community, and she thinks it could be adapted for our situation. The emphasis is on having the young people understand the impact of their actions and make meaningful amends to the community they've harmed."

"And the kids?" Mayor Hendricks asked. "Are they responsive to the idea?"

"More than I expected," Will admitted. "I think some of them are tired of feeling like outsiders, like they don't belong anywhere. The idea of earning their place in the community through service rather than having to fight for respect... it appeals to them."

"That makes sense," she said. "Most people want to belong somewhere. These kids have just been looking for belonging in the wrong places."

"Absolutely," Will said, his enthusiasm growing. "And Mrs. Dosela thinks that if we can show them how to be useful to the community in positive ways, they'll discover they don't need the gang identity to feel important."

Mayor Hendricks finished the last bite of her meal and pushed the bowl away with obvious satisfaction. "This has been exactly the conversation I was hoping to have. Will, I want you to know that you have my complete support for this program. I'll do whatever I can to make sure the city's resources are available to help it succeed."

"Thank you," Will said, and I could hear the genuine gratitude in his voice. "That means a lot."

After the mayor left, promising to keep clearing the roadblocks, I reflected on the conversation while I helped Jacquie finish cleaning the kitchen.

"She seems like good people," Jacquie said, scrubbing down the prep counter with her usual thoroughness. "Not many politicians would take the time to have that kind of conversation with someone like Will."

"I was thinking the same thing," I said, loading the last of the dinner dishes into the dishwasher. "She really listened to what he was saying, and her support seems genuine."

"Plus she cleaned her plate," Jacquie added with a grin. "Always a good sign in my book."

As I drove home through the quiet streets of Nueva Vida, I felt optimistic about the gang situation for the first time in weeks. With Mayor Hendricks backing Will's program and the tribal council enthusiastic about part-nering with the city, it seemed like the Devil Dogs might have a path toward becoming productive members of the community.

It was a reminder that even in the middle of investi-gating a murder, life in small towns continued to move forward. People were still working to solve problems, still caring about their neighbors, still believing that positive change was possible.

The thought occurred to me that Linda Ramos would have approved of the restorative justice approach. As an elementary school teacher, she'd probably seen her share of kids who'd gotten off to rough starts but had the potential to turn things around with the right support and guidance.

Whatever Linda had been investigating at the retreat, whatever had gotten her killed, I hoped we'd figure it out in time to prevent anyone else from getting hurt. Nueva Vida deserved to keep its optimism about human nature and community solutions.

6

I woke Wednesday morning to the sound of my phone buzzing with an excited text from Will: *Big tribal council meeting this morning! Everything's coming together. Can't wait to tell you.*

The enthusiasm in his message made me smile as I got ready for work. After yesterday's revelation about Linda's investigative activities and the mayor's supportive visit, it felt good to know that at least one situation in Nueva Vida was heading in a positive direction.

By the time I arrived at EB Eats, Jacquie was already in full swing with breakfast prep, humming along to the classic rock station while she diced potatoes for her popular hash browns. Her contentment as she worked in her domain always made the diner feel like home.

"Morning, Jacquie," I called, tying on my apron. "Smells incredible in here."

"New seasoning blend for the chili sauces," she said, grinning over her shoulder. "Added a tiny bit of cumin and smoked paprika. Want to try it?"

She handed me a spoon with a small sample of the

sauce, although with the chilies and onions, it was more like a salsa. I had to close my eyes at the complex flavor—the heat of the peppers balanced by the earthy spices and the rich depth of sweetness from the tomatoes.

"That's perfect," I said. "Customers are going to love it."

"Good," she said with satisfaction. "Because I already made a double batch."

The morning rush was steady but manageable, with the usual mix of locals grabbing quick breakfasts and tourists lingering over coffee while planning their day in Nueva Vida. Around ten o'clock, Will burst through the front door with an expression of pure excitement that transformed his usually serious face.

"The meeting was incredible!" he announced, then looked embarrassed by his own enthusiasm. "Sorry, I know you're working, but I had to tell someone."

"Don't apologize, you're not on shift," I said, pouring him a cup of coffee. "I want to hear everything. How did it go with Mrs. Dosela and the council?"

Will settled onto a counter stool, practically vibrating with excitement. "They love the whole program. Not just willing to participate—they're excited about it. Mrs. Dosela said it fits perfectly with their traditional approach to handling conflicts within the community."

I could feel my excitement building. "And the kids? Are they on board?"

"That's the best part," Will said, taking a grateful sip of coffee. "Eddie came to the meeting—you remember Eddie, the one who spoke up at the community meeting? He brought two of the other kids with him, and they actually apologized. Not some fake, forced apology, but a real one. They said they were tired of feeling like outsiders and wanted to find a better way to be part of Nueva Vida."

"That's wonderful, Will. I'm so proud of you for making this happen."

"It's not just me," he said. "Mrs. Dosela did most of the work, explaining how traditional justice focuses on healing the community rather than just punishing individuals. And Mayor Hendricks was amazing—she stood up to some pretty harsh criticism from people who thought the program was too lenient."

"What kind of criticism?"

"The usual stuff—worried about setting bad precedents, concerned that other kids would think they could get away with criminal behavior." Will shrugged. "But the mayor pointed out that our current approach isn't exactly working. We keep having the same problems with different kids every few years."

Jacquie had been listening while she worked, and she looked up from the grill with a smile. "Smart woman, that mayor. Takes guts to try something new when people are scared of change."

"She also asked about Derek's situation," Will said, his expression growing more serious. "Said she was sorry he was going through this and hoped the real truth would come out soon."

I felt a warmth toward Mayor Hendricks that had been growing since her visit yesterday. In a world full of politicians who seemed more concerned with re-election than actual problem-solving, she appeared to be genuinely invested in making Nueva Vida better.

"Did she say anything else about the murder case?" I asked.

"Just that she trusted George and Denise to handle it, but that she knew how hard it was on Derek to have his reputation questioned." Will paused. "She mentioned that she'd been following the investigation in her official capacity and that there were some aspects that didn't make sense to her either."

That was interesting. If the mayor had concerns about the official investigation, it suggested that there might be more complexity to Linda's death than the police were revealing publicly.

Around noon, after the lunch crowd had settled into their comfortable rhythm of conversation and clinking silverware, I texted Kashvi: *Free for a trip to the retreat this afternoon? Want to follow up with Serenity.*

Her response came back quickly: *Perfect timing. Slow day at the bookstore, and I have new questions.*

An hour later, Lissa and Lola were in charge at the diner and we were driving back toward Serenity Springs, the desert landscape looking different in the midday heat. The mountains shimmered in the distance, and the air itself seemed to pulse with warmth and possibility.

"What's your strategy for Serenity?" Kashvi asked, consulting her notebook, where she'd written what looked like a detailed interview plan.

"I want to understand more about Linda's community documentation project," I said. "And I want to know what that argument with Linda was really about."

When we arrived at the retreat, Serenity met us in the same common room as before, but her energy was noticeably different. The flowing earth-tones remained, but her usual serene composure seemed more fragile, like she was working harder to maintain it.

"I'm glad you came back," she said, settling onto the cushioned bench across from us. "I've been thinking about our conversation yesterday, and I realize I wasn't entirely forthcoming about Linda's behavior here."

Kashvi and I leaned forward, sensing that we were about to get the information we really needed.

"Linda wasn't just asking casual questions about people's backgrounds," Serenity continued, her hands twisting in her lap. "She was gathering information about everyone's personal business—financial troubles, professional problems, relationship issues. It was like she was conducting an investigation."

"An investigation into what?" I asked.

Serenity was quiet for a long moment. "I think she was looking for people who had secrets. People who might be vulnerable to... pressure."

"Blackmail?" Kashvi said softly.

"I don't know for certain," Serenity said, waving her hand in dismissal. "But she had this way of asking follow-up questions that suggested she already knew more about people's situations than they'd told her. And she seemed particularly interested in anyone who'd had legal or financial difficulties."

"Including you?" I asked.

Another long pause, this one stretching until I wondered if Serenity was going to answer at all.

"Linda somehow knew that I'd changed my name," she said. "She asked me whether Serenity Walsh was my birth name, and when I tried to deflect, she made it clear that she already knew the answer."

"Is that what you argued about Sunday night?"

Serenity's composure cracked completely. "She said she was writing about people's redemption stories for her project. But the way she asked her questions, the specific details she seemed to know—it felt more like she was gathering ammunition than celebrating people's fresh starts."

I thought about the Linda everyone in Nueva Vida knew

—the beloved schoolteacher who volunteered for every charity drive and never missed a community meeting. This version of Linda, the one who gathered people's secrets and made them feel threatened, was completely different.

"Serenity," I said, "did you feel like Linda was threatening you?"

"Not directly," she said, her voice barely above a whisper. "But she made it clear that she knew things about my past that could damage the retreat if they became public. She suggested that people who'd genuinely changed their lives deserved to have their stories told as inspiration for others."

"But you didn't want your story told?"

"My past isn't the kind of inspiration anyone needs," Serenity said bitterly. "Some things are better left buried."

As we drove back to town, Kashvi and I were both quiet, processing what we'd learned.

"So Linda was definitely investigating people," Kashvi said. "But we still don't know if she was planning to expose them or blackmail them."

"Either way," I said, "someone decided she'd gotten too close to something that had to stay secret."

7

The dinner crowd at EB Eats was just finishing when George and Detective Denise Collett walked through the front door together. The sight of both detectives arriving at the same time made my stomach tighten—in my experience, that meant either wonderful news or terrible news, and their expressions suggested it wasn't the former.

"Evening, detectives," I called from behind the counter, where I was restocking the dessert display with Jacquie's fresh apple turnovers. "Coffee? Dinner?"

"Coffee would be great," George said, settling onto his usual counter stool. Detective Collett took the seat beside him, her posture rigid. I wondered if she ever relaxed or if she was always on duty and ready to take down a perp.

I poured two cups of our evening blend—a smooth medium roast that paired well with dessert—and set them down with cream and sugar. Usually, serving people kept me in my happy place. Tonight, I just felt like I was delaying some kind of old-school interrogation.

"Busy day?" I asked, trying to keep my tone light while I wiped down already-clean surfaces.

"You could say that," Detective Collett said, her voice carrying an edge I didn't like. "We've been following up on some interesting information about Linda Ramos."

"Oh?" I tried to look merely curious rather than guilty of unauthorized investigation. I hadn't passed anything we'd learned so far, which admittedly was something I should have done.

George took a long sip of coffee, then looked at me. "We've been hearing that people around town have been more... forthcoming with certain individuals than they have been with the official police investigation."

My cheeks warmed. "I'm not sure what you mean."

"We mean," Detective Collett said with barely concealed irritation, "that somehow you and your friends have gotten retreat participants to share information they haven't mentioned in their formal statements. Information that might be crucial to solving this case."

"How am I supposed to know what you've found out. And, people remember things after a while, did you re-interview them?" I glanced around the diner as I spoke. The evening crowd was thinning out, but there were still a few customers nursing their coffee and dessert, and the last thing I wanted was for this conversation to become public entertainment. "Could we maybe talk in the back booth?"

George nodded, and we moved to the corner booth that had become our unofficial conference room. The warm lighting and comfortable seats usually made even tough conversations feel more manageable, but tonight the detectives' serious expressions dampened the usual coziness.

"Eliza," George said once we settled, "we know you've

been talking to Emily Stonehouse and Dr. Zhang. And we know they've told you things they didn't mention to us."

"Like what?" I asked, though I was pretty sure I knew where this was heading.

"Like the fact that Linda was asking specific, very invasive questions about people's personal business," Detective Collett said. "Questions that went far beyond normal social interaction."

I decided honesty was the best policy—this time. "Yes, they mentioned that Linda seemed unusually interested in people's backgrounds and financial situations. They felt uncomfortable with how persistent she was."

"And did they tell you why they thought she was asking those questions?" George asked.

I wondered what George and Denise knew. Was it time to tell all or hold back and risk them finding out? "Emily thought Linda was working on some kind of community history project. But both she and Dr. Zhang seemed to think it was more invasive than that."

Detective Collett leaned forward. "What we're finding, Eliza, is that Linda Ramos wasn't the sweet, harmless elementary school teacher that everyone in town believed her to be."

"What do you mean?" I asked, though part of me was already dreading the answer.

George chose his words carefully. "Linda was gathering information about people's vulnerabilities. Financial problems, legal troubles, professional embarrassments— anything that could be used as leverage."

So they did kind of know everything. "Leverage for what?"

"That's what we're trying to determine," Detective

Collett said. "But people rarely collect that kind of information for altruistic purposes."

I thought about Serenity's nervous revelation about Linda's questions, about Emily and Dr. Zhang's discomfort, about the argument Serenity had with Linda the night before she died. "Are you saying Linda was blackmailing people?"

"We're saying," George said, "that Linda appears to have been engaged in activities that made several people very nervous about their secrets becoming public."

The implications of that sank in. If Linda had been threatening to expose people's secrets, then her murder might have been less about random violence and more about desperate self-preservation.

"That changes everything about Derek's situation," I said.

"Yes and no," George said. "Derek still prepared the food that killed her, and he still had access to that food during the critical time period. But if Linda was threatening multiple people, then our suspect pool is much larger than we initially thought."

Detective Collett added more sugar to her coffee and stirred it aggressively. "Which is why we need civilians to stop conducting their own interviews and scaring off suspects or contaminating evidence."

"I understand your concerns," I said, "but people tell me things they wouldn't tell you. Small-town dynamics—"

"Are exactly what we're worried about," Detective Collett interrupted. "If word gets out that we're investigating Linda's activities, people will start destroying evidence or coordinating their stories."

George's approach was gentler but no less firm. "We appreciate your help, Eliza. The information you've shared has been valuable. But from here on out, we need you to let us handle the official investigation."

After they left, I sat alone in the back booth, processing what they'd told me. Linda Ramos, beloved elementary school teacher, had apparently been using her community connections to gather ammunition about people's secrets. Someone had killed her to stop whatever she was planning to do with that information.

And Derek was still caught in the middle, his life and business hanging in the balance while the truth remained hidden.

Jacquie emerged from the kitchen with a piece of her apple turnover with melted cheddar on top and a concerned expression. "Everything okay? You look like someone just told you Santa Claus was running a betting ring."

"Something like that," I said, accepting the pastry. "Turns out our murder victim might not have been as innocent as everyone believed."

"People rarely are," Jacquie said with the practical wisdom that made her such a grounding presence. "The question is whether her secrets were worth killing for."

I bit into the turnover—perfectly flaky crust surrounding sweet, cinnamon-spiced apples—and wondered the same thing. If Linda had been planning to expose corruption or blackmail people with embarrassing secrets, someone had decided murder was preferable to public humiliation.

The cozy warmth of EB Eats surrounded me as I contemplated the growing complexity of the case. Outside the windows, Nueva Vida looked peaceful in the evening light, but underneath that small-town tranquility, someone was walking around free after committing murder.

And I was supposed to pretend I didn't care about finding out who.

8

T he next morning I was trying to figure out how I was going to help Derek and avoid annoying Denise Collett into arresting me. I wasn't giving up the case despite a sleepless night worrying about whether I should or not. Just as I reached for my phone to text Kashvi and Jet, Alistair burst through the front door of EB Eats looking like someone had stolen his bravado. His usual theatrical flair was notably absent, replaced by genuine frustration and what looked suspiciously like embarrassment.

"Coffee," he said without preamble, slumping onto a counter stool with uncharacteristic lack of drama. "Strong coffee. And maybe some sympathy, though I suspect I don't deserve it."

My coffee was superior to his boring brew, but I didn't ask if that was why he'd come. I poured him a cup of our morning blend—dark and robust enough to revive the dead —and set it in front of him along with cream and his preferred raw sugar. "Rough morning?"

"You could say that." Alistair stared into his coffee like it might contain answers to all of life's problems. "I've spent the last two days trying to gather information about Linda's activities, and I've managed to accomplish nothing except convince half of Nueva Vida that the entire McKay family has lost its collective mind."

Jacquie looked up from the grill where she was preparing her breakfast special—scrambled eggs with green chili and cheese that made the whole kitchen smell like heaven. "What kind of information gathering?"

"The detective kind," Alistair said miserably. "I thought if I talked to people around town—Linda's neighbors, fellow teachers, people who might have known what she was working on—I could uncover clues that would help clear Derek's name."

"And instead?" I prompted, though I was already dreading the answer. He'd agreed to let us do the investigating. Why had I believed him?

"Instead, I discovered that people don't trust someone whose cousin is the prime suspect in a murder case. Who knew?" Alistair's voice was heavy with self-recrimination. "Mrs. Patterson actually shut the library door in my face when I started asking about Linda's research habits. And don't get me started on what happened at the elementary school."

I winced. "You didn't try to question Linda's teaching colleagues, did you?"

"I merely made some casual inquiries about her recent behavior and whether she seemed to be working on any special projects." Alistair took a long gulp of coffee. "Apparently, 'casual inquiries' from the murder suspect's cousin are viewed with significant suspicion."

I'd bet it was more his approach than his relationship to Derek. "Alistair," I said, "people are scared and trying to protect themselves. Of course they're not going to share information with someone they see as biased."

"I realize that now," he said. "But Derek is getting more depressed by the day, and I can't just sit around doing nothing while his life falls apart."

The bell over the door chimed again, and Derek himself appeared, scanning the diner until he spotted Alistair at the counter. Unlike his dramatic cousin, Derek moved quietly and seemed to prefer blending into the background rather than commanding attention. He looked tired and pale, like someone who hadn't been sleeping well. Who could blame him?

"Alistair," Derek said, approaching with obvious relief. "I've been looking everywhere for you. Mrs. Patterson called the house and said you were at the library making inquiries about Linda's research habits."

Alistair had the grace to look embarrassed. "I was just trying to help—"

"By questioning librarians about a murder victim?" Derek's voice was firm. "Alistair, you're making things worse. People are starting to talk about the unstable McKay cousins, and that's not helping my case."

I felt sorry for both of them. Derek was clearly trying to salvage his reputation while dealing with his well-meaning but misguided cousin's attempts to help.

"Derek," I said, "maybe there's a different way you could contribute to figuring out what happened. Something that uses your actual skills instead of relying on Alistair's... enthusiasm."

Derek looked curious. "What did you have in mind?"

"Well," I said, refilling their coffee cups, "if Linda was working on some kind of community documentation project, there might be information in publicly available records that could help explain what she was really investigating. Court documents, property records, business filings —the kind of things that require patience and technical skill to search through properly."

Derek's expression sharpened with interest. "I used to be a software engineer—spent eight years working for a tech company in Albuquerque before I decided to follow my passion for food service. I'm very good with databases and research."

"You left tech for catering?" I asked, surprised.

"Best decision I ever made," Derek said with the first genuine smile I'd seen from him. "The tech world was everything I hated—constant pressure, impossible deadlines, people treating each other like disposable resources. Cooking lets me create something that nourishes people. It's honest work that makes people happy."

"But you still have the research skills?"

"Bit rusty, but sure. I might have a few not so legitimate skills too." Derek paused, looking hopeful for the first time since this whole mess started. "It would be better than just sitting around waiting to be arrested again."

Alistair was practically vibrating with renewed enthusiasm. "Derek would be perfect for that! He's methodical, detail-oriented, and much better with computers than I am. Plus, it would keep me from making things worse by interrogating innocent librarians."

"But," I said, looking at Alistair, "this would mean no more amateur detective work on your part. No more questioning townspeople, no more casual inquiries, no more dramatic entrances demanding information from people who don't want to talk to you."

"I understand completely," Alistair said, and for once I thought he might actually mean it. "I'll leave the investigation to the professionals and let Derek handle the research."

"Good," I said. "Because right now, Derek needs to stay as far away from anything that looks like interfering with police business as possible."

Derek grabbed Alistair's elbow and pulled him along to the street.

Just as I was feeling like we'd found a productive direction for the cousins' energy, the bell over the door chimed again and Vic Simons walked in, still wearing his firefighter uniform—and looking good enough to distract every female in the diner.

"Hey, Eliza," he said with that easy smile that always made me feel slightly off balance. "I'm here to pick up the lunch order for the station."

"Right on time," I said, retrieving the bag of sandwiches I'd packed for the fire department. "Jacquie made sure to add extra of that salsa you guys love."

"Perfect. You know how grumpy firefighters get when they don't have good food." He accepted the bag but didn't immediately head for the door. "I was wondering if you'd like to have dinner this weekend. Uncle Brad's been asking when I'm going to bring you by for a proper meal."

I felt my pulse quicken at the invitation. "That sounds wonderful. When were you thinking?"

"Saturday evening around six? Brad's place is just outside town—oh yeah, you know where it is. I can pick you up if you'd like." Vic's expression was casual, but there was something in his eyes that suggested this invitation meant more than just a friendly meal.

"I'd like that," I said, trying to ignore the way my stomach did a little flip of anticipation.

"Great. Fair warning though—Brad's going to want to

hear all about how you solved those other cases. He's been following your detective work with great interest."

After Vic left, promising to call with more details about Saturday, I looked forward to the weekend with an anticipation that had nothing to do with investigating murder. It had been a long time since I'd been genuinely excited about spending time with someone, and the prospect of a relaxed evening with Vic felt like exactly the kind of normal I'd been craving.

"That looked promising," Jacquie said with a knowing grin as she arranged fresh rolls in the warming basket. "About time you had something fun to think about instead of just murder and mayhem."

"It's just dinner," I said, though I couldn't suppress my smile.

"Sure it is," Jacquie laughed. "And I'm just a cook, not someone who's been watching you light up every time that man walks through the door."

As the lunch crowd began filtering in, I thought about the balance between solving Linda's murder and living my life. Derek and Alistair had a constructive plan for research that wouldn't get anyone arrested, Will's gang intervention program was showing real promise, and I had a dinner date with someone who made me laugh.

Maybe Nueva Vida was big enough for both justice and happiness after all.

9

An hour later, Derek's research had already borne fruit. His text to Kashvi and me was brief but alarming: *Emily's financial situation much worse than she admitted. Can you visit her shop? Have specific questions based on what I found.*

Now, Kashvi and I were standing outside Stonehouse Boutique, watching Emily through the window as she rearranged a display of essential oil bottles with the nervous energy that suggested she had too much time to think. Her shop looked even more overwhelming than usual—bottles and jars crowded every surface, and the competing floral scents were visible in the way they made passersby speed up their walking pace.

"Remember," I said to Kashvi as we approached the door, "we're here as concerned friends, not investigators with financial records."

Kashvi held up her phone, where she'd kept Derek's questions to hand. "Got it. Though those aromatherapy fumes might make it hard to think clearly regardless."

Emily looked up when we entered, and I could see the

exact moment she realized this wasn't a casual shopping visit. Her bright smile faltered, and her hands went still on the inventory she'd been obsessively organizing.

"Back again?" she asked, her voice carrying a note of wariness that made my heart ache for her. "I thought we covered everything yesterday."

"Emily," I said, moving closer to the counter, "we've been thinking about what you told us regarding Linda's questions. About your financial situation."

The color drained from Emily's face, and she gripped the edge of the counter like she needed the support. "What about it?"

"We're wondering if there might be more to the story," Kashvi said. "Linda seemed to know very specific details about people's private business."

Emily was quiet for a long moment, then sank onto the stool behind the register. In her cheerful yellow cardigan and careful makeup, she looked like someone playing dress-up as a successful businesswoman.

"She knew everything," Emily said finally, her voice barely above a whisper. "About the loans, about the house being collateral, about the business credit lines. She knew I owed almost sixty thousand dollars across multiple creditors."

I felt my stomach drop. Derek's research had been accurate—Emily was in much deeper trouble than she'd let on.

"How could Linda have known all that?" I asked.

"That's what I kept wondering. She said she was working on a community project about how small businesses were handling economic pressures. But her questions were so specific, so detailed..." Emily's voice shook. "It felt like she'd done research before she ever talked to me."

Kashvi leaned against the counter, her expression sympathetic. "That must have been terrifying."

"It was. She knew about the cash deposits too—the money from selling my grandmother's jewelry. She asked if I'd been reporting it properly to the IRS."

"And had you?" I asked.

Emily's face crumpled. "I should have been more careful about the tax implications, but I needed the money immediately for the mortgage payment. When you're about to lose your house, you don't always think through every consequence."

I understood that kind of desperation. When you're drowning, you grab whatever looks like it might keep you afloat, even if you're not sure it's strong enough to hold you.

"How much money are we talking about?" Kashvi asked.

"About five thousand dollars over the past two months. Antique jewelry that had been in my family for generations." Emily wiped her eyes with the back of her hand. "I know I should have consulted an accountant, but with the IRS already watching me so closely after the last audit..."

My sympathy wouldn't solve the case, so I asked, "What did Linda say about the cash sales?"

"She said she understood the temptation to take short-cuts when you're desperate. But then she started asking whether I knew other business owners who might be in similar situations, whether I'd considered what she called 'more creative solutions' to my problems."

This was worse than I thought. We didn't have to look at the questions Derek sent us. Emily was spilling all the details with just a little prompting. "Creative solutions?"

"She didn't specify, but the way she asked... it felt like she was fishing for information about other people's financial troubles. Like she was building some kind of database."

I exchanged glances with Kashvi. Linda's community documentation project was sounding more and more like an information gathering operation. If I was right in my suspicions, it wasn't for the good of the community, either.

"Emily," I said, "when Linda died, where exactly were you?"

"Still at the retreat until the police released us. I was in my room most of the morning—I'd had trouble sleeping and was trying to meditate." Emily paused. "Why? You don't think I could have killed her, do you?"

"We're just trying to understand the timeline," I said. "But Emily, you should talk to a tax attorney about those jewelry sales. You know from experience there are ways to handle situations like this, and you don't have to face it alone."

"I keep meaning to call someone, but attorneys cost money I don't have. And I'm scared that asking for help will just make things worse with the IRS." She twisted her fingers as if the answer was there just under the skin.

"Sometimes asking for professional help is the only way to make things better," Kashvi said kindly. "I can give you the name of someone who might work with you on payment arrangements."

After we left Emily's shop—with promises to help her find affordable legal advice—Kashvi and I sat in my car for a moment, processing what we'd learned.

"So Linda was definitely gathering detailed information about people's vulnerabilities," I said.

"And Emily was terrified Linda was going to report her new tax problems to the IRS" Kashvi added. "That's a significant motive for wanting Linda to"

"Strong enough to kill for?" I thought so, but maybe I was following a trail that wasn't really there.

"For someone facing bankruptcy and potential criminal charges for tax evasion? Maybe." Kashvi sent Derek a text with what we'd learned.

I started the car and pulled away from the boutique, watching Emily in the rearview mirror as she stood in her doorway looking lost and scared. Whatever Linda was concocting, it had left people feeling threatened and vulnerable.

And someone had decided murder was preferable to exposure.

"We need to talk to Dr. Zhang next," I said. "He needs to tell us the full story, just like Emily did."

10

————

The early evening air was perfect for walking—crisp but not cold, with a golden light that made the desert landscape look like something from a painting. When Dr. Zhang had suggested we continue our conversation on one of Nueva Vida's hiking trails rather than at the diner, I'd been surprised but intrigued. Sometimes people were more comfortable sharing things they'd rather keep hidden when they weren't sitting across from each other at a table.

Jet had volunteered to join me, and I was grateful for his calming presence as we met Dr. Zhang at the trailhead just outside town. With him along, I didn't have to worry about getting lost. The three of us walked in comfortable silence for the first few minutes, the only sounds being the crunch of dry ground under our feet and the distant call of a road-runner somewhere in the scrub brush.

"Thank you for agreeing to meet like this," Dr. Zhang said, pausing at a scenic overlook where we could see Nueva Vida spread out below us in the valley. "After yesterday's conversation at the diner, I realized there are things I should probably tell you about Linda's questions. Things that might help you understand what she was really doing. And I didn't want Emily to hear the details."

I settled onto a flat rock, Jet claiming another nearby, while Dr. Zhang remained standing, his hands shoved deep into his jacket pockets. Even in casual hiking clothes, he carried himself with a professional tightness.

"We're listening," I said.

"Linda wasn't at the retreat for healing or meditation," Dr. Zhang said, staring out at the desert landscape. "She was investigating. A very thorough, very invasive investigation into everyone's backgrounds."

"What kinds of questions was she asking you?" Jet asked. "Be as open as you can. It will help us find the real killer."

"She wanted to know about my medical practice, why I'd left Phoenix, my family background, my financial situation." Dr. Zhang's voice carried a note of weariness. "At first I thought she was just naturally curious—some people are interested in others' stories."

"But it went beyond normal curiosity?" I prompted.

"Much beyond. She had specific questions about my previous work, about why I'd left my position so suddenly, about whether I was properly licensed to practice in New Mexico." Dr. Zhang turned to face us. "She seemed to already know answers to some questions she was asking, like she was testing me rather than learning from me."

A familiar statement. I couldn't think of Linda as a kind person any longer. Dr. Zhang shuffled his feet, stirring up a tiny cloud of ochre dust. The desert evening was settling around us, painting the sky in shades of pink and orange that would have been breathtaking under different circumstances. Tonight, though, I focused on the growing anxiety in Dr. Zhang's voice.

"What was your work in Phoenix?" I asked.

Dr. Zhang sighed deeply, preparing to share a burden he'd been carrying alone. "I was a consultant for ZMS Medi. Not a practicing physician, but someone who reviewed clinical trial protocols and drug safety data." He paused. "The company was later investigated for falsifying research results."

"Were you involved in the falsification?" Jet asked.

"No. Actually, I was the one who first raised concerns about irregularities in the trial data. When the company ignored my warnings and told me to keep quiet, I documented everything and resigned." Dr. Zhang's voice grew bitter. "But try explaining that when your former employer is on the front page of every medical journal for endangering patients with fake research, and no one is interested in guilt or innocence, just drama."

I felt a surge of sympathy for him. "That must have been incredibly difficult."

"I'd spent fifteen years building a reputation as an ethical consultant, and suddenly I was associated with one of the biggest pharmaceutical scandals in Arizona history. Even though I was a whistleblower, the timing made it look like I was fleeing prosecution."

"Is that why you came to Nueva Vida?"

"I wanted a fresh start somewhere I could practice medicine without having to constantly defend my connection to ZMS. I've been working part-time at the clinic here for three years, and it's been wonderful. The community has been accepting, trusting. My patients know me as someone who cares about their health, not someone connected to corporate pharmaceutical fraud."

The sun was setting behind the mountains now, casting long shadows across the desert floor. Dr. Zhang looked smaller somehow, diminished by the weight of sharing his story.

"What did Linda want to know about your pharmaceutical work?" I asked.

"Everything. The specific studies I'd worked on, my role in the company, the timeline of when I left. She said she was working on a project about how people rebuilt their lives after professional setbacks, but her questions felt more like preparation for a criminal case."

"Did she seem to believe your explanation about being a whistleblower rather than a co-conspirator?"

Dr. Zhang shook his head. "I don't think she cared about the truth. She seemed more interested in the appearance of impropriety, the fact that I'd left under suspicious circumstances. She kept asking whether I thought the people of Nueva Vida deserved to know about my background when they trusted me with their medical care."

That sent a chill through me. "She threatened to expose your connection to the pharmaceutical scandal?"

"Not directly, but the implication was clear. She said she believed in transparency and accountability, especially with people in positions of trust." Dr. Zhang's voice grew frustrated. "She made it sound like she was protecting the community from me."

"How did you respond?" Jet stood up and walked to the edge of the overlook, giving Dr. Zhang a moment to compose himself.

"I tried to explain the truth—that I'd been the one who exposed ZMS's fraud, not participated in it. I offered to show her documentation proving my whistleblower status." Dr. Zhang joined Jet at the overlook. "But she said documentation could be fabricated, and that what mattered was public perception."

"How did that make you feel?" I asked, feeling more like a counselor than an investigator—or diner owner, which is what I am.

"Terrified," Dr. Zhang admitted. "I've built a good life here. I have patients who trust me, colleagues who respect my work, a chance to practice medicine the way I always wanted to—helping people instead of serving corporate interests. If Linda had started spreading rumors about my connection to pharmaceutical fraud, it could have destroyed everything."

We walked back down the trail in thoughtful silence, the evening air cooling around us as the desert prepared for night. By the time we reached our cars, I believed that Dr. Zhang was telling the truth about his background—and convinced that Linda's threat to expose him gave him a powerful motive for murder.

"Dr. Zhang," I said as we prepared to part ways, "where were you the day Linda died? Between noon and three o'clock?" If we needed to check people's alibis, the time frame was from Derek delivering the snack and Linda eating it.

"At the retreat until the police released us. I was reading in the common area most of the morning—I'd been too unsettled by my conversation with Linda to participate in the meditation sessions." He paused. "I know how this looks. I had every reason to want Linda silenced. But I'm not a killer. I'm just a doctor who's been trying to rebuild his life after getting caught up in some difficult ethical choices."

As Jet and I drove back toward town, the lights of Nueva Vida twinkling in the valley below, I thought about the difference between guilt and innocence with motive. Dr. Zhang might be telling the truth about not killing Linda, but his fear of exposure was real enough to drive someone to desperate measures.

"What do you think?" Jet asked as we pulled into the EB Eats parking lot.

"I think Linda was playing a dangerous game," I said. "And I think Dr. Zhang is scared of losing the life he's built here."

"Scared enough to kill?"

"That," I said, "is what we need to figure out."

11

Friday morning, Will arrived at opening time with three of the former Devil Dogs members: Eddie, Maria, and a quiet boy named Santos who looked like he'd rather be anywhere else. They settled into our largest corner booth, and I could see Will's gentle coaching as he helped them navigate what was probably their first experience in a sit-down restaurant as welcomed customers rather than potential troublemakers.

Joined them with my order pad and welcomed them in. While I'd like to think I was happy these reforming gang members chose to patronize my diner, there was a little fear in the back of my mind that we'd end up being a gang hangout.

"This is really nice," Maria whispered, running her fingers over the smooth surface of our cheerful table setting. She was maybe fifteen, with heavy-handed makeup that clashed with her youthful look. "I always wanted to eat here, but I thought you wouldn't want people like us."

Great, my guilt spiked. "People like you are who we want," I said, stepping aside so Lissa could put down four cups of hot chocolate topped with whipped cream. "You're part of Nueva Vida's community."

Eddie, who'd spoken at the original community meeting, looked around the diner with obvious appreciation. "It feels different than I expected. Friendlier. More like..."

"Like home?" Lissa suggested before she headed for another table. "That's the whole point of places like this."

Santos, who hadn't spoken yet, finally looked up from his hot chocolate. "Mrs. Dosela said we should practice being part of the community before the official program starts. See what it feels like to belong somewhere positive."

"How's that going?" I asked.

"Better than I thought," Eddie admitted. "Yesterday we helped clean up the playground at the elementary school. Some of the little kids were there with their parents, and they weren't scared of us. They just saw us as big kids helping make their playground nicer."

"That must have felt good," Will said, pride evident in his voice.

"It did. Different than the feeling you get from making people nervous," Maria agreed. "This was like... useful energy instead of nervous energy."

Her insight struck me. These kids were clearly capable of deep thinking about their choices and their impact on others.

"Mrs. Dosela told us something interesting yesterday," Eddie said, glancing at Will, "about Ms. Ramos—you know, the teacher who died."

My attention sharpened. "What about her?"

"Mrs. Dosela said she used to volunteer with after-school programs for at-risk kids. But she stopped coming around about two years ago, right when some of us were starting to get into trouble." Santos spoke quietly, but his words carried weight. "She said it was like Ms. Ramos lost interest once the kids got too difficult to help."

Will nodded. "Mrs. Dosela was careful about how she said it, but the implication was that Linda Ramos wasn't as committed to helping kids as people thought. She was good with the straightforward cases—the kids who just needed encouragement. But with the ones who really needed help, who had serious problems at home..."

"She gave up on them," Maria finished bitterly. "Left them to figure it out alone."

I felt a chill as another piece of Linda's true character emerged. The beloved schoolteacher who everyone thought cared about all children, had abandoned the ones who needed her most. I didn't regret losing that image. "That's not the Linda Ramos everyone talks about," I said.

"No, it's not," Will agreed. "And Mrs. Dosela said she'd noticed other things over the years. Linda was great at organizing fundraisers and charity events, but she always made sure her name was prominently associated with the successful projects. The ones that didn't work out... somehow other people got blamed for those."

After the kids finished their hot chocolates and left, promising to meet Will later for their community service assignment, I reflected on this new information while I helped Jacquie prepare for the lunch rush.

"Sounds like your murder victim was more complicated than people realized," Jacquie observed, chopping vegetables for her lunch special. "Amazing how death makes everyone forget the unpleasant parts of a person's character. Until something comes along to loosen their tongues."

"It's making me wonder what else we don't know about Linda," I said.

After the encouraging morning with the gang kids, I

looked forward to what felt like the first genuinely productive lead we'd had in days. Serenity had called the diner
around noon, her voice urgent. "I need to talk to you," she'd
said without preamble. "About Linda, about what she was
doing at the retreat. Can you come this afternoon?"

Now, Jet and I were driving back to Serenity Springs, the
familiar desert landscape looking different in the bright
afternoon sunlight. The mountains stood sharp against the
blue sky, and the air itself seemed to shimmer with heat and
possibility.

"Think she's finally ready to tell us the truth?" Jet asked,
adjusting his sunglasses against the glare.

"I hope so. We've got three people with motives, but we
still don't understand what Linda was trying to accomplish."

When we arrived at the retreat, Serenity met us at the
door looking nothing like the serene wellness guru we'd
encountered before. Her flowing earth-tones had been
replaced by jeans and a simple t-shirt, her long blond hair
pulled back in a messy ponytail, and she looked like she'd
been crying.

"Thank you for coming," she said, leading us to the
common room. "I should have told you this from the beginning, but I was scared. Scared of what people would think,
scared of losing everything I've built here."

We settled onto the familiar cushioned benches, but the
atmosphere was different from our previous visits. The crystals still caught the light, and the inspirational quotes still
decorated the walls, but without Serenity's carefully maintained spiritual presence, the room felt like a stage set
waiting for the actors to return.

"Serenity," I said, "whatever Linda was doing, we need to
understand it to figure out what happened to her." I thought
about telling her that Dr. Zhang and Emily had been brave

enough to talk, but decided it felt wrong without their permission.

"Linda was blackmailing me," Serenity said, the words tumbling out like she'd been holding them back for too long. "And probably others too, but I can only speak to my own experience."

Jet leaned forward. "What did she have on you?"

Serenity took a shaky breath. "My real name is Sarah Walsh. I changed it legally five years ago when I opened the retreat, but it wasn't just for spiritual reasons like I told people. I changed it because I was running away from who I used to be."

"What do you mean?" I asked.

"In high school and college, I was terrible. The worst kind of popular girl who made other students feel worthless just to maintain my social position. I said cruel things, organized exclusions, made people's lives miserable because I thought it made me powerful." Serenity's voice grew smaller with each word. "I was a bully. Not just mean—actively, systematically, cruel to people who didn't deserve it."

I felt a surge of sympathy for her, not that her victims didn't deserve the same, but Serenity was hurting. "That must be difficult to live with."

"It was destroying me. I had what you'd call a spiritual crisis in my late twenties—realized that everything I thought made me important was just making me a terrible person. So I changed everything. Studied meditation, learned about compassion, devoted my life to helping people heal instead of causing them pain."

"And Linda found out about your past?" Jet asked.

"She'd done extensive research. She knew specific incidents—things I'd said to particular students, ways I'd humiliated people, even some of the worst moments that I'd blocked from my memory." Serenity met my eyes. "She talked to people I'd hurt, gotten detailed accounts of how my behavior had affected them."

"What did she want from you?" Jet asked.

"At first, she said she was documenting redemption stories for her community project. But then she started asking for things. Free retreat weekends for families she recommended, special meditation sessions for her volunteers, donations to her charity events." Serenity's voice grew bitter. "When I hesitated, she'd mention how disappointed my current clients would be to learn about Sarah Walsh's behavior."

So no longer a vague idea that Linda was blackmailing people. I wondered what she'd gotten from Emily and Dr. Zhang. "How long had this been going on?" I asked.

"About six months. It started small—just a weekend here and there for people who couldn't afford it. But Linda kept escalating her requests, and the threats became less subtle." Serenity stood up and walked to the window, staring out at the meditation garden, something she seemed to do when needing time. "She said she believed in accountability and that people who'd harmed others shouldn't get to escape consequences just because they'd changed."

"But you had changed," Jet said.

"I know that. And most days, I believe it. But Linda had a way of making me feel like I was still that horrible teenager, just hiding it better." Serenity turned back to face us. "She said that true redemption required facing the full consequences of your actions, not just changing your name and hoping people forgot."

"That must have been terrifying," I said.

"It was. Fifteen years of trying to make amends, fifteen years of building this place where people can find healing, and she could have destroyed all of it by sharing what she'd learned about my past." Serenity's voice broke. "My clients trust me because they see me as someone who's found peace. If they knew about the cruelty I was capable of..."

Well, I did understand Linda's rationale. How could anyone know someone really changed? But Linda wasn't judge or jury. Serenity's actions should be proof enough. "Did she threaten to expose you publicly?"

"She said she was writing a comprehensive report about Nueva Vida's approach to handling people with problematic pasts. She wanted to document whether the community was being naive about giving people second chances." Serenity returned to her seat, looking smaller somehow. "She specifically mentioned that my story would be a central case study."

"A case study in what?" Jet asked.

"Whether people who'd caused significant harm to others deserved to rebuild their lives without facing ongoing consequences. Whether communities should trust reformed bullies with positions of spiritual authority." Serenity's hands twisted in her lap. "She made it sound like an academic study, but the way she asked her questions, the specific details she seemed to know... it felt like preparation for a public flogging."

"When did you realize she was blackmailing you rather than just documenting your story?"

"The night before she died. She seemed excited about something, kept checking her phone and making notes. When I asked what had her so energized, she said her research was coming together in ways she hadn't expected." Serenity's voice grew quieter. "She said she was looking forward to having some meaningful conversations about truth and accountability with several community leaders."

"Several?" I asked. "Not just you?"

"That's what scared me the most. Linda had been investigating multiple people, and she seemed to be planning some kind of coordinated exposure. Like she was building toward revealing everyone's secrets at the same time."

I exchanged glances with Jet. If Linda had been planning to expose corruption or embarrassing secrets involving multiple prominent community members, that would explain why someone had been desperate enough to kill her.

"Serenity," I said, "the morning Linda died—what were you really doing?"

"I told you, I was in my office working on scheduling and trying to figure out how to handle all the free services Linda had demanded I provide. I heard someone scream and came running." She paused. "I know how this looks. I had every reason to want Linda silenced. But I've spent fifteen years learning to resolve conflicts without violence. I couldn't go back to destroying people just to protect myself."

Jet pulled out his phone, and I noticed he started a text to Derek and Kashvi. This was one of the more complicated updates so far.

"Do you think Linda was planning to expose everyone she'd been investigating?" I asked.

"I think Linda believed she was protecting the community by forcing people to be accountable for their past actions. But I also think she didn't understand the difference between justice and revenge." Serenity looked around the peaceful room that represented years of trying to become a better person. "Sometimes the kindest thing you can do is allow people's mistakes to stay in the past, especially when they've genuinely tried to make amends. Linda was more like the old me than she was willing to admit."

As we drove back toward town, I thought about the complexity of human nature. Serenity had been cruel as a teenager but had transformed herself into someone who helped others heal. Did her past mistakes disqualify her from her present good work?

"What do you think?" Jet asked as Nueva Vida came into view.

"I think Linda was playing a dangerous game with people's lives," I said. "And I think someone decided they'd rather commit murder than face whatever she was planning to expose."

"But which someone? Emily facing financial ruin, Dr. Zhang losing his medical career, Serenity having her spiritual transformation questioned—they all had reasons to want Linda stopped."

"Or someone else entirely," I said. "Someone we haven't identified yet who had even more to lose."

———

12

Derek came through the front door, carrying his laptop bag and grinning like he'd made a significant discovery. He looked more energized than I'd seen him since this entire ordeal began, like finally having a constructive way to contribute to solving his own case had given him new purpose. The dinner rush was in full swing, but there was a free stool at the counter.

"Evening," I called from pointing to the seat. I was restocking the napkin dispensers and condiment bottles so Lola and Lissa could work the tables. "How's the research going?"

"Better than expected," he said, settling onto his usual stool. "Much better since I got your updates on the interviews. Man, why do people take so long to admit the full truth? I've been diving deeper into the pharmaceutical scandal Dr. Zhang mentioned, and if this was an example of how she worked, Linda's investigation was more extensive than any of us realized."

Jacquie emerged from the kitchen with a plate of her evening special—green chili chicken enchiladas that filled the air with the tangy aroma of roasted peppers and melted cheese. "I'm sure this will cheer you up," she told Derek. "You look you've been staring at a computer screen all day."

"You're not wrong," Derek said gratefully, accepting the steaming plate. "But I've found some things that change our understanding of what Linda was doing."

I poured him a glass of soda and settled onto the stool beside him, grateful that I didn't have to serve customers. "What did you find?"

Derek pulled out his laptop and opened it to a screen full of official-looking documents. "Dr. Zhang wasn't just a consultant who worked for a pharmaceutical company that got in trouble. He was the primary whistleblower who exposed ZMS's fraudulent clinical trials."

"That sounds like he was a hero, not a criminal," I said. "And he didn't brag about his role. So I don't think he was looking for credit."

"But here's what's interesting—Linda had copies of internal company emails that show Dr. Zhang received death threats from ZMS executives after he went public. He didn't just leave Phoenix for a fresh start; he left because he was genuinely afraid for his safety."

I felt a chill. "And Linda knew about the death threats? How would she get that information?"

"She had documentation of everything. The FBI investigation, the witness protection considerations, even Dr. Zhang's new identity papers when he moved to New Mexico." Derek took a bite of his enchilada and shook his head. "Maybe she's a secret hacker, or is forcing someone to give her files."

"But if that's true, then his fear of Linda exposing him makes even more sense," I said. "If word got out about his connection to ZMS, the people who wanted him silenced might find him here."

"That's a pretty powerful motive for wanting Linda to keep quiet," Derek agreed. "But there's more. I also found records showing that Dr. Zhang has been practicing without a current New Mexico medical license."

He hadn't mentioned that. "What do you mean?"

"His license expired two months ago, and he never renewed it. I guess he didn't want anything to lead his previous employers to him. Technically, every patient he's treated since then has been seen illegally." Derek showed me an official document on his screen. "If Linda had reported that to the state medical board..."

"He would have faced criminal charges for practicing medicine without a license," I finished. "On top of being found by the people who wanted to hurt him in Phoenix."

"Exactly. Dr. Zhang had multiple reasons to want Linda's investigation stopped."

Jacquie, who had been listening while she cleaned her prep station, looked up with concern. "Poor man. Sounds like he was trying to help people and got caught up in other people's corruption. I mean, it's not like all his knowledge and experience goes away if his license isn't current."

"Because I'm working with data, I can see the bigger picture," Derek said. "I'm pretty confident that Linda was investigating people who'd made mistakes or gotten caught up in situations beyond their control, but she wasn't distinguishing between victims and criminals."

"What do you mean?" I asked. Criminals would certainly complicate the investigation.

"Well, take Serenity's situation. Yes, she was cruel in high school, but she genuinely changed and has spent fifteen years helping people heal. Dr. Zhang exposed corruption and saved patients from dangerous drugs, but he's been labeled as suspicious because of his connection to the scandal." Derek paused. "Linda seemed to think that any kind of complicated past disqualified people from having respected positions in the community."

I thought about our conversation with Serenity that afternoon, her fear that her clients would lose faith in her guidance if they knew about her teenage cruelty. "So Linda wasn't just blackmailing people for services—she was positioning herself as the moral authority who decided whether people deserved their second chances."

"That's how it looks to me," Derek said. "And that's a very dangerous position to put yourself in, especially in a small town where everyone has something they'd rather not have exposed. And everyone thinks they know how people should live their lives."

The bell over the door chimed, and Will walked in carrying a sheaf of papers and wearing an expression of barely contained excitement.

"Perfect timing," I told him. "Derek's been updating us on his research findings. We need some positive news. How did the gang program meeting go this afternoon?"

"Incredibly well," Will said, settling onto the stool on Derek's other side. "The kids are excited about their community service projects, and Mrs. Dosela thinks the program could be a model for other communities. But..." He paused, his expression growing more serious. "Mrs. Dosela confirmed what Eddie said about Mrs. Ramos."

"What did she say?" I asked. "It helps to hear it without Eddie filtering the news."

"Mostly just specifics. She said Linda used to volunteer with after-school programs for at-risk kids, but she stopped coming about two years ago. Right around the time some of the Devil Dogs members were starting to get into real trouble." Will's voice carried a note of disappointment. "Mrs. Dosela was careful about how she said it, but the implication was clear—Linda was good at helping kids who were easy to help, but with the ones who needed support..."

"She gave up on them," Derek finished.

"Exactly. She left them to figure things out on their own when they became too difficult or time-consuming." Will shook his head. "It's making me wonder if Linda's community service reputation was more about looking good than helping people."

I exchanged glances with Derek. "That fits with what we're discovering about her investigation. She seemed more interested in documenting people's failures than helping them succeed."

"Speaking of which," Derek said, returning to his laptop, "I have more news. I found something else that's troubling. Linda had been researching city employees and officials, not just private citizens."

"What kind of research?" Will asked.

I hoped he wasn't planning a career as an amateur investigator.

"Contract histories, budget allocations, vendor relationships—the kind of deep dive that would uncover financial irregularities if they existed—maybe if they didn't." Derek pulled up another screen. "She'd identified patterns that suggest corruption going back years. Maybe it's in the interpretation, but maybe it's real. From what we've found, Linda wouldn't care either way."

"Political corruption?" I asked, though I was already dreading the answer.

"That's what it looks like. And based on the timeline of her research, she was planning to present her findings to someone in authority. She'd scheduled meetings for the week after she died."

"Meetings with whom?" I asked.

Derek's expression grew grave. "I'm still working on that. But if Linda had discovered evidence of corruption involving current city officials, then we're not just dealing with blackmail anymore. We're dealing with someone who killed to cover up crimes that could send them to prison."

After Will left to prepare for the weekend's community service activities and Derek headed back to Alistair's house to continue his research, I cleaned the diner with extra thoroughness, my hands needing something to do while my mind processed everything we'd learned.

"You're thinking hard about something," Jacquie observed, wiping down the grill. "Sounds like the case is getting more complicated?"

"Much more complicated," I said, organizing the coffee station for the third time, handing a condiment pack to Lissa as she passed to deliver an order. "We started out thinking this was about retreat participants with embarrassing secrets, but it's looking more like Linda was investigating serious crimes involving people with genuine power in this community. Maybe not just here."

"That's dangerous territory," Jacquie said. "You don't want to be getting in the way of something that big."

"I know. And I'm starting to worry that we're getting in over our heads." I paused in my restocking to look at her. "Linda was killed to stop her from exposing something. If we get too close to that same information..."

"Then you make sure the police know everything you've learned, and you don't go anywhere alone," Jacquie said firmly. "Nueva Vida needs people like you, Eliza Burton. Don't let some corrupt official take that away from us."

13

Saturday morning started with another urgent text from Derek: *Found more about Emily's financial schemes. Plus Linda's city records requests are suspicious. Can you meet at Alistair's by 9 AM?*

I arrived to find Derek's laptop surrounded by even more papers than usual, and Alistair pacing around his ornate living room with obvious agitation.

"Derek's been up since dawn," Alistair announced. "I barely managed to get him to eat breakfast before he disappeared back into those confounded records!"

"What did you find?" I asked, accepting the coffee Derek offered me.

"Emily's MLM work. I checked them after you sent me the information about her selling off family heirlooms. The schemes go deeper than just aromatherapy oils," Derek said, pulling up a series of business registration documents. "She's been involved in at least six different multi-level marketing companies over the past three years. Jewelry, supplements, kitchen products, skincare—all of them failed, and all of them left her deeper in debt."

"How much debt are we talking about?" I asked, trying to ignore Alistair's pacing.

"The sixty thousand we already knew about, plus another thirty in MLM inventory she can't move and business loans for marketing packages that never generated income." Derek clicked to another tab. "But here's what's interesting—Linda had documentation of all of it. Not just the current situation, but the entire history of Emily's failed business ventures."

"How could Linda have known about all that?" I asked.

"That's where it gets concerning. Linda had been systematically accessing public records for months. Business registrations, tax filings, bankruptcy proceedings, court documents." Derek showed me a spreadsheet that made my head spin. "She wasn't just researching the retreat participants—she was investigating dozens of Nueva Vida residents. I haven't found her source, but there's a locked folder I haven't been able to hack yet."

I felt my stomach drop. "Dozens?"

"Anyone with any kind of public profile or community involvement. Business owners, city employees, nonprofit leaders, teachers. She'd requested access to twenty years of city archives for her historical documentation project."

"But those records weren't historical," I said, not understanding where this was heading.

"Recent contracts, budget reports, vendor payments— the kind of information you'd need to uncover financial irregularities." Derek's expression grew grave. "Linda wasn't writing Nueva Vida's history. She was building a case for massive municipal corruption."

Alistair stopped pacing. "Good heavens. No wonder someone killed her. If she'd discovered evidence of city officials stealing money..."

"That's not even the worst part," Derek continued. "I tracked Linda's research timeline, and she was building toward something specific. She'd scheduled meetings for the week after she died with several city officials."

"Including who?"

"I'm still working on that, but one name keeps appearing in her notes." Derek hesitated. "Patricia Hendricks processed payments for most of the questionable contracts during her early years with the city."

The room went silent as the implications sank in. Mayor Hendricks, who had seemed genuinely supportive of Will's gang program, who had appeared concerned about Derek's situation, was connected to twenty years of municipal corruption.

"Are you certain about this?" I asked.

"The public records? Yes, there's a clear trail. Patricia was a county clerk from 2003 to 2007, then moved to city hall as a contract administrator until 2010. Most of the financial irregularities Linda identified happened during those years." Derek pulled up another document. "And here's what's really troubling—Linda found a pattern of contract modifications that were approved without proper documentation, all of them processed by Patricia's department."

A phone call from Vic interrupted the morning research session, reminding me about our dinner plans with his Uncle Brad. After promising Derek we'd meet tomorrow to discuss the corruption findings with the full team, I spent the rest of Saturday trying to focus on normal activities while my mind churned through what we'd learned.

By six o'clock, I was driving out to Brad's ranch house with Vic, grateful for the distraction of what promised to be a relaxing evening. Brad met us on his front porch, looking exactly as gruff and opinionated as I remembered, but with a welcoming smile that suggested he'd been looking forward to company.

"About time you two showed up," he said, though there was warmth in his voice. "Barbacoa's been slow-cooking since dawn, and I don't want to hear any complaints about the heat level."

"It smells incredible," I said, and I meant it. The rich aroma of spices and slow-cooked beef filled the evening air.

Brad's house was comfortable and lived-in, with family photos covering the walls and furniture chosen for durability rather than style. It felt like a place where conversations happened over good food.

"Hope you're hungry," Brad said, leading us toward the kitchen. "I've got enough food for an army, and some stories about this town that might interest you."

Over dinner—which was indeed incredible despite being almost too spicy to eat—Brad regaled us with tales of Nueva Vida's development over the past thirty years. He'd been involved in local politics as a young man, and had worked on several of the construction projects that had shaped the town's current infrastructure.

"Those were interesting times," he said, refilling our glasses with beer that helped cut the heat from the barbacoa. "Lot of money flowing through city government, lot of decisions being made without as much oversight as we probably should have had."

"What do you mean?" I asked, though I suspected I knew where this was heading.

"Well, take those road improvements from the early 2000s. Budget said they should cost maybe three hundred thousand, but the final bills were closer to six hundred thousand. Change orders, emergency repairs, additional materials—always something that drove the costs up."

"Was that normal for construction projects?" Vic asked.

"Some cost overruns are normal, but the pattern was concerning. Always the same companies getting the contracts, always the same types of 'unexpected complications' that justified higher payments." Brad took a long drink of his beer. "I mentioned it to some people at the time, but I was told the city administration had everything under control."

I thought about Derek's research, about Linda's systematic investigation of city records. "Did anyone ever look into those irregularities?"

"Not officially. But funny you should ask—Linda Ramos was here about six weeks ago, asking very similar questions about those old construction contracts."

My pulse quickened. "What kinds of questions?"

"She said she was working on a project about Nueva Vida's development. Wanted to know about the decision-making process, who was involved in approving the big contracts, whether there were any community concerns about cost overruns." Brad's expression grew thoughtful. "I thought she was just being thorough about the town's history."

"But now?" Vic prompted.

"Now I'm wondering if she found something that worried her. Her questions were very specific—not just about what happened, but about who had access to financial records, who would have had the authority to approve questionable payments."

"Did she seem concerned about anything specific?" This was exactly the kind of lead we needed to find our killer. Or maybe just feel more confident in our assumptions.

Brad hesitated. "She asked about Patricia Hendricks. Said she was interested in Patricia's early career with the city, how she'd worked her way up from clerk to mayor. Linda wanted to know about Patricia's role in processing those contracts, whether she'd had concerns about the financial irregularities."

I felt a chill. "What did you tell her?"

"That Patricia was young then, probably just doing what her supervisors told her to do. But Linda kept pushing—digging into Patricia's access to budget information, whether she would have seen the patterns of cost overruns."

"And would she have?"

"Patricia processed payments for most of the major contracts during her time as a clerk. She would have seen everything—the original budgets, the change orders, the final payments that were often double what was approved." Brad met my eyes. "If there was something suspicious happening, Patricia would have been in a position to know about it."

"Did you tell anyone about Linda's visit?" I asked.

"I mentioned it to Patricia a few weeks later when I ran into her at the hardware store. Told her someone was asking questions about the old construction contracts, thought she should know in case it was something the city needed to address officially."

That might have been the first step on a path that led to murder. I didn't mention it. Brad had done what he thought was right. "How did she react?"

"She seemed concerned. Thanked me for the heads-up and said she'd look into it. Asked what Linda was planning to do with her research." Brad refilled our plates with more of the incredible barbacoa. "I told her Linda had been vague about her intentions, but that she seemed very focused on documenting everything thoroughly."

"What did you think Linda was up to?" Vic asked.

Brad was quiet for a moment, choosing his words carefully. "I thought she was just being a thorough historian. But looking back, some of her questions made me wonder if she was more interested in finding problems than in documenting solutions." He paused. "She asked a lot about who benefited from those contracts, where those people are now, whether they'd used their positions for personal gain."

"That sounds more like an investigation than historical documentation," I said.

"That's what I'm thinking now. And if Linda found evidence that city officials had been involved in corruption..." Brad's voice trailed off as the implications became clear.

As we drove back to town through the quiet Saturday evening, Vic and I were both subdued by what we'd learned.

"You think Mayor Hendricks could be involved in municipal corruption?" Vic asked.

"I don't want to believe it," I said honestly. "She's been so supportive of Will's program, so concerned about Derek's situation. But if Linda found evidence connecting her to questionable contracts..."

"That would be a pretty powerful motive for murder," Vic finished. "I don't like the idea of you walking into such a dangerous situation."

"I'll be careful." I stared out at the lights of Nueva Vida twinkling in the valley below, wondering how many other secrets our peaceful small town was hiding, and whether we were smart enough to uncover the truth before someone else decided we knew too much.

14

———

I was barely in the door from my dinner with Vic and Brad when my phone buzzed with an urgent group text from Derek: *Need team meeting ASAP. Got into Linda's locked folder. This changes everything. Alistair's house, 8 PM.*

By the time I arrived at Alistair's, Kashvi and Jet were already settled in the familiar living room, which had been transformed into a professional investigation headquarters. Derek had papers covering every surface, multiple laptops open, and a timeline taped to one wall that stretched from floor to ceiling.

"It's taking you far too long to prove Derek's innocence," Alistair snapped at me before offering tea. He leaned in and added in a whisper, "I want my home back, and this mess gone."

"It takes what it takes," Derek said, his quiet intensity more pronounced than I'd ever seen it. "This might speed things up. I finally cracked Linda's password-protected files. What I found is bigger than anything we imagined."

I accepted the tea Alistair offered and settled into the only unoccupied chair. "How much bigger?"

Derek turned his laptop screen toward us, showing a comprehensive database. "I was right about the extent of her blackmail. But most of it is petty stuff, no one would kill over it. But, dozens of people were on her list."

"That many?" Kashvi asked, her notebook already open.

"Business owners, city employees, nonprofit leaders, teachers—anyone with a community reputation worth protecting." Derek clicked through file after file. "She'd created detailed profiles on everyone's vulnerabilities and was using that information to extract services, money, and cooperation."

"What kinds of services?" Jet asked.

"You know about Dr. Zhang providing free medical care for families Linda referred to him. Serenity was giving free retreat weekends to Linda's chosen participants. Emily was providing access to customer financial information through her credit card processing records." Derek's voice grew grim. "To be honest, those are the petty ones I mentioned."

"Maybe small, but I don't think any of them would say their problems were petty," I said. I dreaded the answer, but had to ask, "what were the bigger ones?"

"Linda had files on at least fifteen local business owners who were providing significant financial support for her community documentation project. Construction contractors, restaurant owners, retail shops—all of them paying what amounted to protection money to keep Linda from exposing their tax irregularities, licensing violations, or past mistakes. Reputation might be a motivator, but for these people, I'd guess money was stronger."

Alistair nearly dropped his teacup. "You're saying Linda was essentially running a protection racket?"

"That's exactly what I'm saying. She'd positioned it as community fundraising for historical preservation and charitable work in her files, but really she was using people's shame and fear to fund her lifestyle and her investigation activities. It's all here. The police will be busy sorting it out."

I thought about Brad's description of Linda's questions, her interest in who had benefited from the questionable city contracts. "Do we think all of this was building toward exposing the political corruption?"

"That's where it gets interesting," Derek said, pulling up another set of files. "Linda had been documenting twenty years of questionable city contracts, cost overruns, and suspicious vendor relationships. I couldn't believe how deep she went. Her sources were in code, but I'm sure given enough time someone will crack it. But I worked out that she wasn't planning to turn this information over to authorities."

"What do you mean?" Kashvi asked. "Why would she keep it... Oh yeah, money."

Derek nodded and pointed to the laptop. "Based on her notes and correspondence, Linda was planning to use the corruption evidence as leverage against city officials. She'd identified several current and former employees who could be implicated in the financial irregularities, and she was preparing to approach them directly. Like she was going to form her own kind of shadow government. It all sounds way too far out there. "

"For what purpose?" Jet asked, though I suspected we all knew the answer. "I mean beyond the money. Nueva Vida isn't important enough for a conspiracy. And what was she planning to make the elected officials do?"

"The same purpose as everything else—to extract cooperation, funding, and control," Derek said to stop Alistair pontificating. "Linda had discovered that municipal corruption was much more profitable than blackmailing individual business owners. I guess she had a vision for our town. She didn't record it, though."

The room fell silent as the full scope of Linda's activities sank in. She hadn't been investigating corruption to expose it or to help the community heal from past mistakes. She'd been building a case to use against people for her own benefit.

"That's monstrous," Alistair said. "Using people's past mistakes—even their efforts to do the right thing—as weapons against them. Taking over our town like some tin pot dictator? She teaches our children for heaven's sake!"

"It gets worse," Derek continued. "I found evidence that Linda had already approached at least one city official. Someone had been making regular payments into an account Linda controlled, payments that were labeled as historical consultation fees."

"Who?" I asked, though I had a sinking feeling I knew.

"The payments came from an account associated with Patricia Hendricks. Five thousand dollars a month for the past four months."

"Mayor Hendricks paid Linda twenty thousand dollars?" Kashvi said, her voice rising.

"It looks that way. And based on Linda's calendar, she had a meeting scheduled with someone identified only as P.H. for the Monday after she died. The notation says 'final discussion, terms adjustment.'"

Alistair jumped up, beginning to pace around his own living room. "Now wait just a minute! Are we seriously suggesting that our mayor—a woman who has been nothing but dedicated to this community—was being blackmailed by Linda Ramos?"

"The evidence suggests—" Derek began.

"The evidence suggests nothing definitive!" Alistair interrupted, his dramatic nature asserting itself. "Patricia Hendricks has supported every positive initiative in this town! She backed that gang program when others wanted those kids locked up. She's been gracious and professional in every interaction. And we're going to accuse her of corruption and murder based on some old paperwork and suspicious payments?"

"Alistair," I said, "we're not accusing anyone. We're trying to understand what Linda found and why someone killed her for it."

"Well, what Linda found could destroy an innocent woman's life!" Alistair's voice grew more passionate. "Young city clerks don't question their supervisors' decisions. Patricia might have just been processing payments she was told to process, following procedures she was trained to follow."

Why was he defending her so emphatically? Had he forgotten Derek was accused of the crime? One that the mayor had a better motive for committing?

"But the payments to Linda suggests—" Kashvi began.

"The pattern suggests that Linda was a manipulative blackmailer who destroyed people's lives for personal gain!" Alistair spun around, gesturing dramatically. "And if Patricia was paying her, it might have been because Linda was threatening to spread lies about her involvement in twenty-year-old corruption she had nothing to do with!"

I nodded. "That's actually a fair point. Even if Mayor Hendricks was innocent of any wrongdoing, having Linda spread rumors about corruption could still destroy her career. And Linda threatened that with other people."

"Exactly!" Alistair sank back into his chair as if he'd used up all his energy in the performance of his outrage. "Linda could ruin someone's reputation regardless of whether they'd done anything wrong. The mere suggestion of corruption would end a political career."

"So Mayor Hendricks could be a victim of Linda's blackmail rather than a participant in corruption," Jet said.

"Which would still give her a powerful motive for murder," Derek pointed out. "If Linda was demanding more money or threatening exposure despite the payments..."

"Then Patricia might have decided murder was preferable to public disgrace," I finished.

We sat in contemplative silence for several minutes, processing the awfulness of what we'd discovered. Linda hadn't been the beloved community member everyone thought she was—she'd been a systematic manipulator who used people's past mistakes against them. And Mayor Hendricks might be either a corrupt official or an innocent victim, but either way, she had compelling reasons to want Linda silenced.

"There's something else," Derek said. "Sorry. I should have thought about this and given you all the information. I found email exchanges between Linda and someone she refers to only as Subject One. The emails suggest this person was planning to do something drastic to stop Linda's investigation."

"What kind of drastic?" I asked.

"The last email, dated two days before Linda died, says: 'This has gone far enough. I won't let you destroy everything I've worked for. We need to meet and resolve this permanently.'"

"That is a threat," Kashvi said. "I mean does anyone think it isn't?"

"Of course it sounds like a threat to someone looking for

a motive! It could be a plea for negotiation," Alistair said. "Someone desperate to find a peaceful solution before Linda destroyed their life. If that was really going on!"

"Do we have any idea who Subject One is?" Jet asked.

Derek shook his head. "Linda was careful not to use real names in her most sensitive correspondence. But the timing and the language suggest this person was her primary target —the person she was planning to expose or blackmail most extensively."

"Mayor Hendricks," I said.

"Possibly. But without more evidence, we're still just speculating." Derek closed his laptop, looking exhausted by the weight of what he'd discovered. "What we do know is that Linda was a much more dangerous person than anyone realized, and that someone decided murder was preferable to whatever Linda was planning."

15

I'd started opening the diner for Sunday breakfast. Most people were at church, so it was quieter than the weekday rushes, with a relaxed atmosphere that made it feel more like a neighborhood gathering than a restaurant. I wasn't sure if I'd make it permanent, but I enjoyed the peaceful rhythm of serving coffee and Jacquie's weekend specialty—French toast with spiced strawberries that had customers driving from three towns over.

George pushed the door open, and Detective Collett walked in behind him. The sight of both detectives arriving together on a Sunday morning made my stomach tighten. George wasn't here for social reasons with his partner in tow. In my experience, that usually meant either very good news or very bad news, and their serious expressions suggested it wasn't the former.

"Morning, detectives," I called, wiping my hands on my apron. "Coffee? Jacquie's French toast is exceptional today."

"Coffee would be great," George said, settling onto his usual counter stool. Detective Collett took the seat beside him, her posture rigid suggesting I was right; this was official business rather than a social visit.

I poured two cups and set them down along with cream and sugar. The familiar ritual of serving coffee usually calmed my nerves, but today it felt like preparation for a load of bad news.

"How's the investigation progressing?" I asked, keeping my tone light while I organized the already clean coffee station.

"That's what we wanted to discuss with you," George said, his voice carrying a warning note I hadn't heard before. "We've had a complaint about nosy amateur detectives." He smiled to soften the words.

My pulse quickened, but I tried to maintain an expression of innocent curiosity. "Oh?"

Detective Collett leaned forward with a grin of satisfaction. "Serenity Walsh called the station yesterday afternoon. She said you'd been back to the retreat multiple times, asking very specific questions about Linda Ramos's activities and relationships with other participants. She felt harassed by your nosiness."

Wow, it sounded like Serenity was slipping back into her old bullying ways. "We were just trying to understand what happened at the retreat. Derek's still under suspicion, and—"

"And we've told you to leave the investigation to the professionals," Detective Collett interrupted, her voice carrying the edge of patience worn thin. "This isn't some cozy mystery story, Eliza. This is a real murder case with serious legal consequences."

George shot his partner a warning look, then turned back to me with a more diplomatic approach. "What Detective Collett is trying to say is that we're concerned about civilian involvement in an active investigation. Especially when that investigation might be more complex than it initially appeared."

"More complex how?" I asked, though I suspected I knew exactly where this conversation was heading. Why couldn't George trust me to be safe?

George and Detective Collett exchanged one of those looks that conveyed an entire conversation between law enforcement partners.

"Let's just say that Linda Ramos wasn't documenting Nueva Vida's charming local history," Detective Collett said, her tone dry enough to parch the desert. "Her research interests were somewhat more... contemporary and controversial."

"The kind of research that could upset some very important people," George added. "People with significant influence in the community."

I felt a familiar chill as the implications became clear. They knew about Linda's corruption investigation, but they were proceeding cautiously—because accusing elected officials required ironclad evidence and delicate handling.

"That does sound serious," I said, trying to keep my voice neutral because I felt a wave of guilt that I hadn't kept them up to date. My excuse, if I needed one, was that things were happening fast.

"It is serious," George confirmed. "Which is why we need everyone to be extremely careful about spreading rumors or making accusations without absolutely solid evidence to support them."

I kept my eyes on the coffee station, hoping to avoid being caught out. "You know people will gossip even without fuel."

"The thing is," Detective Collett said, stirring what seemed like an excessive amount of sugar into her coffee, "when civilians start conducting their own investigations in cases like this, they can inadvertently damage evidence, contaminate witness statements, or even put themselves in significant danger."

"Danger from whom?" I asked, though I figured I could guess the answer.

"From people who have a great deal to lose if certain information becomes public," George said. "People with power, connections, and the resources to protect themselves by whatever means they deem necessary."

The weight of that implication settled over our conversation like a heavy blanket. They weren't just worried about us interfering with police work—they were genuinely concerned about our safety. But George could have come to tell me this without his partner along. All Denise did to try to get me to stop investigating just made me more determined.

"Look," George continued, "I know you care about Derek McKay, and I know you've been helpful in previous cases. But this situation is unique. If Linda Ramos was killed to cover up financial improprieties involving city government, then we're dealing with someone powerful who has already committed murder to protect their secrets."

"And someone like that won't hesitate to eliminate additional threats," Detective Collett added with grim certainty.

I topped off their coffee cups. "What exactly do you want us to do?" I asked.

"Stay away from this investigation," Detective Collett said immediately. "Stop questioning potential witnesses, stop visiting people connected to the case, and definitely stop playing amateur detective."

George's approach was gentler but no less firm. "We want you to be safe, Eliza. And we want to ensure that when we do make arrests, the case isn't compromised by improper evidence gathering or witness contamination."

"But what about Derek?" I asked, voicing the concern that had been driving our investigation from the beginning. "He's still under a cloud of suspicion, and people around town are starting to whisper about him. His business reputation is being destroyed while he waits for this to be resolved. He's done nothing wrong and yet it sure feels like he's being punished."

"Derek McKay is no longer our primary suspect," George said, which was the first good news I'd heard about the case in days. "We're actively pursuing other possibilities now."

"What kind of possibilities?" I pressed. "And if he's not your primary suspect, why isn't he released form the bail?"

"The kind we absolutely cannot discuss in an ongoing investigation," Detective Collett said, her tone suggesting that line of questioning was closed. "And we release people when we have the actual killer in custody. Derek McKay is not in jail, he just can't leave town. Not a big hardship."

I fought to keep my response inside. Derek's business could collapse while the police waited for permission to arrest a powerful person like the mayor.

They finished their coffee in silence, the weight of their warnings settling around us like morning fog. As they prepared to leave, George paused at the counter and looked at me. "Eliza, I want you to understand that I'm genuinely concerned about your safety. If Linda was killed because she discovered something that powerful people wanted to keep hidden, then anyone else who gets too close to that same information could be at serious risk."

"We're not children," I said.

"I know," George said. "But next time we might not be able to set up a safe way to catch someone if you are there. Don't rush into a confrontation. I need you alive."

I refused to make any promises beyond not doing anything stupid. It seemed to satisfy George, but maybe because he knew I'd be lying if I promised to stop.

After they left, I stared at their empty coffee cups and wondered just how deep we'd gotten ourselves into dangerous territory. The police knew about Linda's corruption investigation, but they were proceeding with the caution that came with accusing people in power—a process that required perfect evidence and careful political navigation.

I was still processing the conversation when Kashvi arrived for our planned Sunday research session, her turquoise hair catching the morning sunlight as she settled onto a counter stool.

"I saw George and Detective Collett leaving," she said, studying my expression. "They looked about as cheerful as tax auditors conducting surprise inspections."

"They weren't," I said, summarizing the warning conversation.

"So they know about the corruption investigation, but they want us to back off completely," Kashvi said. "What do you think we should do?"

I refilled her coffee cup while I considered our options. "I think we need to be extremely careful about our next steps. But I also think Derek deserves to have people fighting for his innocence, people who aren't constrained by political considerations and bureaucratic procedures."

"So we keep investigating, but we're much more cautious about it?"

"Exactly. And we definitely don't share any more information with the police until we know precisely what we're dealing with and who we can trust." Until we had a plan, I had no idea what precautions we needed.

16

By the time we gathered in Alistair's home that evening, I was buzzing with stress and excitement —and, to be honest, a healthy dose of fear. We needed to get our proof today. If we could put it all together, we'd close the case. Or, I guess we could decide to give it all to George so the police could close the case.

"More tea?" Alistair asked, hovering near Derek's shoulder with his favorite china service. The scent of Earl Grey had become the permanent aroma of this investigation. "I've also got some excellent shortbread cookies from the bakery if anyone needs sustenance for continued intellectual endeavors."

"I'm fine," Derek said absently, his fingers flying across the keyboard. "It must be here... wait, I think I've got the final piece we need."

Jet looked up from where he'd been studying timeline notes on the whiteboard, stretching to relieve what had to be a serious crick in his neck. "Please tell me it's something that makes sense of all these clues and alibis, because I'm starting to dream about dates and financial reports."

"Better than numbers," Derek said, satisfaction clear in his voice as he turned his laptop screen toward us. "Linda had multiple layers of security on her files, and I cracked the last of the passwords. What I found changes everything we thought we knew about her investigation."

Kashvi set down her teacup and stood behind Derek, looking at his screen. "What could do that?"

Derek pulled up a complex organizational chart, with names connected by color-coded lines. "Linda wasn't just documenting corruption. She was documenting what appears to be a systematic blackmail operation that she was running herself. Look, it's like a corporate year end report."

I struggled to understand the importance. "Blackmail?" I asked. "We already know about that, what's different?"

"Look at this," Derek continued, pulling up another document that looked like Linda's personal notes, hand-written and scanned. "She had detailed files on dozens of Nueva Vida residents. Not just their secrets, but careful documentation of how she was using those secrets to control their behavior. We knew about it, but now we have proof."

Alistair had stopped his tea-serving routine and was now peering over Derek's shoulder along with the rest of us. "I can't believe I was holding onto hope Linda was really the dear, caring creature we thought."

"I'm not sure I believed she really lived such a double life," Derek said grimly. "But it's all here. Take Emily, for example. Linda had documented Emily's MLM failures, her tax troubles, her previous financial irresponsibility—and it goes back years. But she wasn't planning to expose Emily. She was using Emily's access to customer financial information to research other potential targets." He pointed to the list of steps Linda used to dig into the data Emily gave her.

"And Dr. Zhang?" Kashvi asked, though her expression suggested she was already guessing the answer.

"Yep, we were right. Linda knew about his medical license issues, his desperate need to rebuild his reputation. But instead of reporting him, she was blackmailing him into providing free medical care to families who couldn't afford it." Derek scrolled through more documents. "Serenity too. Linda had evidence of her past actions and it wasn't just free spa treatments. She took the same customer information from Serenity."

Jet shook his head in disbelief. "We thought she was just making people do good deeds. It's not right, but I guess I thought it wasn't so bad. But she was going for money too?"

Derek hit print on the list of retreat clients. "She was building a network of sources who were too scared to say no to her demands for information and cooperation. It doesn't matter if she wanted money or not. That's blackmail."

"Why are you printing?" Alistair asked. "That will take too long, and use up too much paper and toner—you know that smell gives me a headache. Just make a file to send to the police."

Derek ignored his cousin and continued to select files to print. "If I print the proof, the cops can't trace how I got it. Maybe I crossed a line or two by hacking Linda's cloud account."

"You know," Kashvi said, clearly still thinking through the moral implications, "it sounds like Linda was helping people in some ways. Her methods were completely wrong, but I'm sure the families who got free medical care are better off than they would have been otherwise. They won't get that now."

"Oh, well, when you put it that way," Alistair said, waving his teacup in a gesture so dramatic I was genuinely worried for his Persian rug, "I suppose we should nominate Linda for sainthood! Here lies Linda Ramos, who only blackmailed people into doing good deeds!"

"That's enough Alistair, we're helping you, remember." Jet put his arm around Kashvi's shoulders. "If Linda stopped there I might agree, but she didn't. She was setting up a blackmail ring for money. Dr. Zhang can still offer free services, and renew his license before he does. He can get protection from the threats. Emily is always in trouble from her get-rich-quick schemes. And Serenity's reputation? It will survive if she helps others."

"There's stuff here about the mayor," Derek said, cutting off whatever Alistair was about to say. "The corruption research on Mayor Hendricks differed completely from her other blackmail schemes. Linda had documented systematic theft from about 2003 to 2008, but it all stopped around the time Patricia transitioned from city clerk to running for office. Everything still points to Patricia being a scapegoat."

He pulled up a detailed timeline marked with different colored highlights. "Linda was digging around for proof that Mayor Hendricks' political campaign was funded by the people who benefited from the irregularities."

"So Linda knew Patricia had been involved in corruption twenty years ago, but she also knew Patricia was probably not guilty of the crime," Jet said. "But there was money involved. The people who donated to the campaign were not suspicious, right. Just the connection."

"And that's where it gets really complicated." Derek pulled up Linda's calendar. "Linda's appointment schedule shows she wasn't planning to expose Patricia directly. She was planning to blackmail her too."

The room fell silent except for the gentle ticking of Alistair's antique mantel clock.

"Blackmail her into what?" I asked.

"The appointment labeled 'P.H. - final discussion' was scheduled for the Monday after Linda died. But her preparatory notes suggest she was planning to offer Patricia a deal. Keep supporting community programs, keep being a political reformer, keep using her position to help Nueva Vida, and Linda would keep the twenty-year-old corruption evidence buried forever."

I stared at the screen, trying to process the moral complexity of what Linda had been planning. "She was going to blackmail the mayor into being a good public servant? That's where she started with everyone. Good deeds, then some way to make money."

"Yes." Derek shook his head with a mixture of admiration and revulsion. "She thought she was protecting the community by controlling the people in it. Somehow she got greedy and found a way to justify getting paid."

Alistair was pacing now. "So Linda wasn't trying to expose corruption for the sake of justice—she was trying to become the puppet master of Nueva Vida! Using everyone's secrets to control their behavior like some sort of benevolent dictator!"

"I wouldn't call it benevolent," Derek said, closing several of the files he'd been showing us.

"Well, no, but you have to admit there's a certain twisted logic to it," Alistair continued, warming to his theme as he often did when he found a particularly dramatic angle. "If you can force corrupt politicians to be honest and selfish doctors to provide charity care, aren't you technically improving society? It's rather like being a vigilante for moral behavior! Like Robin Hood?"

"I don't remember any tales of Robin Hood terrorizing people," I pointed out, thinking about Emily's obvious distress during our interviews, Dr. Zhang's nervous defensiveness, Serenity's fear of exposure.

"Details, details," Alistair said with an airy wave of his hand that made his teacup tremble precariously. "And as Derek said, this changes everything. We must get a confession."

"Or give this to the police," Derek said. "Linda made a mistake that got her killed. She thought she could control Patricia the same way she controlled Emily and Dr. Zhang and all the others. But Patricia had too much to lose and too much power to be controlled by someone else's agenda. We're not facing down a killer."

"This isn't as good as a confession," Jet said. "We've made assumptions, not many but enough to weaken the case. I don't agree that we run out and confront Mayor Hendricks, but handing this to the cops isn't going to speed them up."

17

Derek's words brought us to a halt. I hadn't thought about it that way. "Let's just take a pause," I said. "Clear our heads." When everyone agreed, we split up. Kashvi and Jet went for a walk around the block. Alistair announced he'd clean the kitchen. Derek walked to the printer and started organizing all the papers.

I moved to the window seat to let the view clarify my thoughts. The evening light outside Alistair's windows was fading now, and I could see neighbors walking their dogs and children riding bikes in front yards—all the normal Sunday evening activities of a peaceful community. Meanwhile, we sat here unraveling the murder committed by the woman they'd all trusted to lead and protect them.

I felt the tension in the room dissipate as I let the thoughts drift. The shortbread and tea weren't enough food —okay, maybe they were enough, just the wrong kind. "We should order dinner," I said.

Derek looked up from the folder he was creating for George to use in the official case. "Good idea." He used his phone to order.

Kashvi and Jet returned a few minutes later. Jet, holding up two bottles of wine, said, "We need a little change of direction."

Alistair set the table, the pizza arrived, and we sat away from the piles of papers and timelines. Real plates, crystal wine glasses, all contributed to the atmosphere of family and coziness.

I finished my first slice before restarting the conversation. "Let's review and someone needs to challenge our assumptions."

"I'll do that," Alistair announced. "I prefer to think of Mayor Hendricks as a good person."

"Okay. First she had the resources to learn everything she needed to know about what Linda was doing. Even how she'd changed from good deeds to money," Kashvi said. "As mayor, she'd have access to information about city contractors, including Derek's background check and references. She'd know about his partnership with the retreat center, his catering procedures, Linda's dietary preferences."

"So would Serenity!" Alistair said. "And any number of people. After all Linda found out the same information."

"True," I said. "It's still not enough to make us believe the mayor is innocent."

Derek wiped his hands on a linen napkin. "She's clearly intelligent and detail-oriented. Twenty years of successfully covering up financial crimes, even if she didn't commit them, requires careful planning and flawless execution. Planning a murder would use the same skill set."

"But Patricia stood behind the whole program for those annoying gang kids," Alistair said. "Doesn't that count for anything?"

"We're not saying she's a completely bad person," I said. "She made a bad choice." A horrible realization struck me like a physical blow, and I felt my stomach drop toward my shoes. "Oh god. Tomorrow."

"What about tomorrow?" Derek asked.

"The gang celebration. Will said Mayor Hendricks is going to be the guest of honor at the community celebration tomorrow afternoon. She's giving the keynote speech about community healing, restorative justice, and the power of second chances."

"We're going to have to sit there and watch a murderer give a speech about justice and community healing?" Jet asked, his voice incredulous.

"While Derek is still under suspicion for the crime she committed," Kashvi added, her voice tight with anger on behalf of her friend.

"And while she takes credit for the gang mediation program that Will and the tribal council developed and implemented through months of patient work," I said, feeling sick to my stomach.

"Well, that does complicate things rather extraordinarily," Alistair said. "I mean, we can hardly leap up in the middle of her speech and shout *J'accuse!* like we're in some sort of Victorian courtroom drama, though the theatrical appeal is undeniable."

"We need to call George," I said, reaching for my phone with shaky hands. "Tonight. Right now. This can't wait until after tomorrow's celebration."

"With what evidence?" Derek asked, and I could hear the frustration and fear in his voice. "We still don't have enough for them to arrest her right away. Twenty-year-old financial irregularities that stopped decades ago? Linda's blackmail files that suggest Patricia was a victim rather than a perpetrator? Circumstantial connections between payment schedules and campaign contributions?"

He gestured at the papers and laptop that represented hours of painstaking research. "Patricia's a sitting mayor with an exemplary record for the past fifteen years and the complete trust of the community. George would take our concerns seriously, but he'd need concrete proof before he could move against someone in Patricia's position. Accusations against a popular elected official require absolute certainty, not educated guesses."

"Derek's right," Kashvi said, though I could see it pained her to admit it. "George would listen to us, but he'd need enough evidence to convince a prosecutor. What we have now is suggestive, but it's not conclusive."

"But we can't just sit through tomorrow's celebration pretending everything's normal," Jet protested, voicing what we were all thinking. "Watching her accept praise for community leadership and restorative justice while knowing she's a murderer? I honestly don't think I can do that convincingly."

I looked around at my friends—people who'd spent an entire exhausting day working to save Derek and find justice for Linda. They were right on both counts. We needed stronger evidence before we could make formal accusations that would stick, but we couldn't wait much longer without risking our own safety or our sanity.

"Alistair are you still unconvinced?" I asked.

"No. With regret, I think Mayor Hendricks is the murderer. And I wish we could simply remove her from office."

"I don't think anyone else is in danger," I said. "If we wait one more day, the celebration goes ahead. We attend tomorrow's event. We observe Patricia carefully without revealing our suspicions, and maybe we can get her to say or do something that will give us the proof we need. But we start gathering the final pieces of evidence immediately afterward."

"And if she realizes we suspect her?" Derek asked the question we were all thinking but hadn't wanted to voice.

"Then we tell George immediately, circumstantial evidence or not, and hope it's enough to keep all of us safe until the proper investigation can begin." I assumed one or both of the detectives would be in attendance.

Alistair refilled his wineglass with the air of a man preparing for the performance of his lifetime. "Well, this should make for an interesting community celebration. Congratulations on the successful gang mediation program, Mayor Hendricks. Lovely speech about the power of second chances and community healing. By the way, did you happen to murder Linda Ramos with poisoned energy bars to avoid being blackmailed for the rest of your political career?"

"Alistair," I warned, but I could hear the nervous laughter in my voice that suggested I wasn't entirely immune to the dark humor of our situation.

"I know, I know. Discretion is absolutely key to our survival," he said with wounded dignity. "But you must admit, the dramatic irony is rather overwhelming. Tomorrow we'll celebrate justice with the very person who perverted it most completely."

I was suddenly desperate to be home in my own space where I could think through everything we'd learned without the weight of group expectations. The woman who'd spent twenty years building a reputation as a caring politician had committed murder to avoid being controlled.

"One more day," I repeated, more to convince myself than anyone else as I headed for the door. "Then we finish this."

18

The celebration of success seemed really premature to me, but Will said the idea was to mark all the milestones. "We've been working on it for a month," he told me. "Mrs. Dosela wanted to show some progress before we talked to the community. So now, we have results to prove they were right in supporting us."

I tried not to think about their biggest supporter being a murderer while I packed my contribution to the potluck lunch—green chili quesadillas with salsa on the side. It didn't seem fair to cast such a dark shadow over what should be a hopeful community celebration, but after this morning's revelations about Linda's blackmail operation and Patricia's deadly motives, I couldn't shake the feeling that we were walking into a performance where the star performer was also a blow to the reputation of everyone involved.

The community center was packed despite it being a Monday afternoon—families who'd rearranged work schedules, tribal council members in their best clothes, city officials, and curious residents who'd heard about the program's remarkable early success. The energy in the room was festive, with colorful balloons and a banner that read "Community Healing Through Justice" stretched across the front wall. Five kids, including Eddie, stood together in a corner, no adults standing with them.

Mayor Hendricks was holding court near the refreshment table, animated and glowing as she described the program's impact to a small crowd of admirers that included several city council members and a reporter from the Nueva Vida Tribune. She was wearing a deep blue blazer that brought out her eyes and projected the confident authority that had made her so popular with voters over the years.

"The key was treating these young people as community members who'd lost their way, rather than criminals to be punished," she was saying to a group that included Mrs. Dosela from the tribal council. "Sometimes the most radical thing you can do is believe in someone's capacity for growth and change."

I studied her face as she spoke, looking for signs of guilt, deception, or the strain of maintaining a false persona while under suspicion for murder. But all I saw was genuine enthusiasm and authentic care for the community and the young people who'd benefited from the program. If Mayor Hendricks was indeed Linda's killer, she was either completely lacking in conscience or one of the most skilled actresses I'd ever encountered. I tried to stop the trickle of doubt that came from deep in my mind.

"Eliza!" I turned to see Will approaching with a plate of food in his hand, looking happier and more relaxed than I'd seen him since the whole gang situation began several weeks ago. "Perfect timing. We're about to hear from the participants themselves, and I think you're going to be amazed by how much they've grown. I can't believe there's such a big turnout."

I followed him toward the front of the room, where the five teenagers had joined their tribal council mentors. They looked nervous but hopeful—clean clothes, combed hair, and most importantly, the posture that suggested they felt they belonged in this room with these people. It was a far cry from the sullen, defensive group that had slouched into their first mediation meeting.

Mrs. Dosela stood to introduce them, her weathered face beaming with pride. "Eddie here is going to speak for the group tonight," she said. "He's comfortable sharing what this experience has meant to all of them."

Eddie, the boy who'd spoken up during our initial community meeting and surprised everyone with his thoughtfulness, stepped forward to address the crowd. At fifteen, he still had some growing to do, but today at least, he stood, shoulders back and clear-eyed.

"Until a couple weeks ago, we thought the only way to matter was to make people afraid of us," he said, his voice a bit shaky but determined. "We figured if we couldn't get respect, at least we could get attention. But Mrs. Dosela and the other elders taught us that real power comes from being useful to your community, not from being a threat to it."

Mrs. Dosela beamed at him from the front row, and I could see several other tribal council members nodding. "Tell them about your community service project, Eddie," Mrs. Dosela said.

"We've been working with the maintenance crew at the elementary school this week," Eddie continued, gesturing to his fellow former gang members with obvious pride. "Painting murals in the hallways, fixing playground equipment that was getting dangerous, helping with the school garden. The little kids wave at us now when they see us coming, instead of running away."

The crowd murmured approvingly, and I caught Mayor Hendricks wiping away what looked like a genuine tear. Her emotional response seemed authentic—either the teenagers' transformation truly moved her, or she was one of the most accomplished manipulators I'd ever encountered.

"The program works because it treats the root causes instead of just the symptoms," Mayor Hendricks said when it was her turn to speak. She moved to the front of the room with the confident ease of someone who'd given hundreds of speeches, but her words carried personal conviction rather than political polish. "These young people didn't need harsher punishment—they needed connection, purpose, and adults who believed in their potential even when they couldn't see it themselves."

She paused, looking at the teenagers with genuine warmth. "What you've accomplished in these past two weeks proves that second chances aren't just about forgiveness—they're about recognizing that people can grow beyond their worst moments and become something better than anyone ever imagined."

The irony of those words, coming from someone who I believed murdered Linda to hide her own worst moments from twenty years ago, wasn't lost on me. I wondered if guilt motivated the mayor's passionate support for second chances over her own hidden past, or if she truly believed in redemption despite being unwilling to face the consequences of her own actions.

"Detective Collett," Mrs. Dosela called out, "would you like to share your observations about the program?"

Detective Collett stood, clearly uncomfortable being put on

the spot at what was a celebration of an approach she'd initially opposed. "I'll admit I was skeptical about this restorative justice approach," she said, her voice carrying its usual no-nonsense tone. "I believed in swift consequences, in making sure young people understood there were real prices for poor choices."

She paused, looking at the former gang members with something that might have been respect. "But I was wrong. These kids didn't need harder consequences—they needed better opportunities and adults who were willing to invest in their futures. The transformation has been remarkable, and I'm glad we tried something different."

The surprise and conviction in her voice suggested that Detective Collett's conversion to restorative justice principles had been hard won. She wasn't someone who changed her mind easily or admitted mistakes lightly, which made her public acknowledgment even more meaningful.

George spoke next, and his comments focused on the broader community impact of the program. "Calls about vandalism and petty crimes are down significantly this week, but more importantly, we've started building genuine trust between young people and law enforcement that will benefit our community for years to come."

As the formal presentations concluded and people began mingling over the potluck refreshments, I joined Cassidey near the dessert table, where several people were loading their plates with an impressive array of homemade treats.

"You made it out of that life," I whispered, watching Eddie patiently explain the playground renovation project to a group of elementary school parents who were hanging on his every word.

Cassidey nodded, her expression more mature than her

sixteen years. "Will did too, and he had to take a beating from his old crew for leaving. But looking at these kids, maybe someday they'll have dreams worth fighting for instead of just fighting. I guess this program is giving us what our parents should have, right?"

"Parents are only people. There's no way to know who'll be good at it." Despite the last words, I felt a warm glow of pride at how much she'd grown in just the past week. "You both did the hard work. We just provided the space for it to happen."

"That's what this program does for these kids," she said, gesturing toward the celebration with a wisdom that continued to surprise me. "It gives them space to be better than their mistakes."

As the afternoon wound down and people began bundling up leftover food to take home, I talked with Mayor Hendricks near the coat rack. Up close, she looked tired despite her obvious happiness about the program's early success, and I couldn't help but wonder if the exhaustion came from maintaining a false persona while under the strain of keeping deadly secrets.

"Thank you for speaking at that first community meeting," she said warmly, her voice carrying what seemed like genuine gratitude. "Your support helped convince some skeptics who thought we were being too soft on crime."

"It was easy," I replied, studying her face for any hint of deception or guilt. "Will's transformation and his commitment to helping others spoke for itself."

"That's what I love most about this kind of justice," Mayor Hendricks said, her voice carrying the conviction that made her such an effective politician. "It recognizes that people are so much more than their worst choices. Everyone deserves a chance to make things right and prove they can be a better citizen."

The conversation felt surreal. Here I was, discussing redemption and second chances with someone who killed to protect herself from facing consequences for choices she'd made twenty years ago. The cognitive dissonance was almost overwhelming.

"Mayor Hendricks," I said, choosing my words with extreme care, "do you think there are limits to forgiveness? Some mistakes that are too serious for second chances?"

Her expression grew thoughtful, and for a moment I wondered if I'd pushed too hard. "That's a profound question, Eliza. I think... I think the capacity for redemption depends on someone's willingness to face the consequences of their actions and work to make amends." She paused, and her next words sent a chill down my spine. "But running from the truth, or hurting others to avoid accountability? That makes redemption much harder to achieve."

I felt my blood run cold at her words. Was she speaking in generalities about justice and accountability, or was this her way of acknowledging what she'd done to Linda? The statement could be interpreted either as the hard-won wisdom of someone who'd learned from experience, or as a subtle justification for eliminating threats to hidden secrets.

As I drove home through Nueva Vida's quiet evening streets, passing houses where families were settling in for Monday night routines, I thought about the complex moral landscape we'd stumbled into. The gang resolution program was working, transforming not just the teenagers involved but the entire community's approach to juvenile justice.

Mayor Hendricks had helped to make it happen. But commitment to other people's redemption didn't give her the right to protect her past. In fact, someone who understood the power of second chances might be more motivated to cover her own mistakes, thinking she would be more a leader if she wasn't an example.

By the time I'd fed Macchiato and settled in at my kitchen table with a cup of tea, I'd decided about our next steps. Tomorrow, we'd take everything Derek had discovered to George. It was time to let the police handle confronting Nueva Vida's beloved mayor about her connection to Linda Ramos's death.

19

My phone rang at six AM on Tuesday, jolting me out of a restless sleep filled with dreams about community celebrations ruined by zombies. Derek's name flashed on the screen, and for a panicked moment I wondered if he'd been arrested again or if Mayor Hendricks had somehow discovered our suspicions.

"Derek?" I answered, my voice thick with sleep and worry. "What's wrong?"

"I'm sorry to wake you so early, but I've been up all night going through Linda's files again. I can't seem to settle this nagging doubt I have. I mean she's risking so much if she gets caught. I guess I can't make sense of it. I'm glad I did because I found something," Derek's voice was urgent. "Can you meet at Alistair's this morning? We need to talk before we do anything else."

I sat up in bed, suddenly wide awake despite the early hour. Yesterday's gang celebration had ended with our decision to take our evidence about Mayor Hendricks to George today, but Derek sounded like he'd discovered something that would change our plans. "How big of a change are we talking about?"

"The kind that might save an innocent person from being destroyed," Derek said. "And the kind that might put us in more danger than we realized."

Two hours later, after the fastest opening routine I'd ever managed at the diner—leaving Jacquie to handle the morning rush with explicit instructions to call if anything went wrong—I was walking into Alistair's dining room to find our unofficial research team looking more somber and exhausted than I'd ever seen them. Derek had his laptop open as usual, but instead of his typical neat stacks of organized printouts, there were just a few key documents spread across the mahogany table.

The morning light streaming through the tall windows seemed somehow different today—harsher, less forgiving than the gentle illumination that had accompanied our previous discoveries.

"Thank you all for coming so early," Derek said, getting straight to the point. "I know we agreed yesterday to take what we had about Mayor Hendricks to the police, but I spent all night going through Linda's files one more time, and I found something crucial that we missed."

Kashvi, who was already settled with her notebook and looked like she'd had about as much sleep as Derek, looked up with concern. "What kind of something are we talking about?"

"Evidence that Mayor Hendricks might not be our killer after all," Derek said, his words falling into the room like stones into still water.

Alistair, who had been uncharacteristically subdued, suddenly perked up with dramatic flair. "I told you! I told you Patricia Hendricks was too fundamentally decent a person to commit murder! Didn't I say we were jumping to conclusions based on circumstantial financial evidence?"

"Did you actually say that?" I asked, relaxing into what I thought of as my usual chair—OMG, I didn't need a favorite chair at Alistair's house. "Because I remember you being pretty convinced about the corruption connection."

"Well, I may have been swept up in the moment," Alistair admitted with wounded dignity. "But deep down, I always had reservations about Patricia being capable of murder. She's been committed to community service for decades!"

"What exactly did you find, Derek?" Jet asked, cutting through Alistair's retrospective wisdom.

Derek turned his laptop screen toward us, his expression serious. "I was trying to find some final concrete proof about the mayor's involvement. Something that the police could use without having to go through time wasting process, when I discovered something that changes our entire understanding of her role in the corruption. Look at this timeline, and don't ask about the legality of how I accessed some of these older city employment files."

He clicked through several documents that looked like internal city records from twenty years ago. "The financial irregularities in city contracts ran from 2003 to 2008, just like we established. Patricia Hendricks started as a county clerk in 2003, moved to processing city payments in 2004, and was promoted to a supervisory role in 2006."

"So she was definitely involved in handling the payments," Kashvi said.

"Yes, but here's what I missed before because it was buried in a list of unconnected files." Derek pulled up what looked like an internal complaint report with official city letterhead. "In late 2005, Patricia filed a formal complaint with her supervisor about irregularities in the payment processing system. She documented specific concerns about inflated invoices, questionable change orders, and what appeared to be systematic overpayments to certain contractors."

I leaned forward, studying the document. "She was trying to stop the corruption?"

"It certainly looks that way. Her complaint was thorough, documenting dates, amounts, and patterns that suggested deliberate fraud. But the complaint was ignored, and she was told to process payments as directed by her superiors." Derek scrolled through more documents. "Linda used a naming convention to hide these files. When I noticed, I found the rest. Linda found copies of follow-up emails where Patricia continued to raise concerns even after being told to drop the issue."

"What happened to those continued complaints?" Kashvi asked as she scribbled notes.

"They were buried and dismissed. Patricia's supervisor at the time was Jeb Alderbrite—the assistant city manager who was later promoted to city manager before retiring with full honors in 2015." Derek's expression grew grimmer. "Alderbrite told Patricia that questioning established payment procedures was above her pay grade and that she needed to focus on processing paperwork, not analyzing it."

"So she was caught between doing her job and doing the right thing," I said, understanding dawning.

"And here's the crucial part that changes everything— Linda's notes show she understood perfectly well that Patricia had been a victim of the corruption, not a perpetrator. She wrote that Patricia had been manipulated and silenced by superiors who used her clerical position to legitimize systematic theft."

Alistair stood up and began his familiar pacing, gesturing with his coffee cup in a way that suggested his dramatic instincts were overriding his morning restraint. "So Patricia was an innocent junior clerk who tried to do the right thing and was told to shut up and follow orders by corrupt supervisors! And twenty years later, Linda was going to use Patricia's forced compliance to blackmail her into continued good behavior? That's even more morally reprehensible than we thought!"

"Actually," Derek said, his voice carrying a note of relief mixed with new worry, "I don't think Linda intended to blackmail Patricia at all. That's where we went wrong."

We all stared at him in surprise. The entire foundation of our theory about Mayor Hendricks being the killer had been built on the assumption that Linda was planning to use the corruption evidence as leverage.

"What do you mean?" I asked. It felt like we were starting the investigation over from the beginning.

"Look at Linda's appointment calendar one more time, but with this context." Derek pulled up the familiar scheduling software. "The entry for the Monday after she died says P.H. - final discussion. But I found her detailed preparation notes for that meeting in a different password-protected folder."

He clicked to another document that looked like Linda's handwritten meeting agenda. "She wasn't planning to confront Patricia with evidence of corruption to control her future behavior. She was planning to give Patricia copies of all the evidence she'd compiled against Jeb Alderbrite and ask for Patricia's help in exposing him."

"Alderbrite?" Kashvi looked up from her notes with confusion. "But he's been retired for nearly ten years now."

"Retired with a full pension, excellent benefits, and a

community reputation as an effective city manager who modernized Nueva Vida's infrastructure during his tenure," Derek said. "But Linda had documented that he was the one orchestrating the entire corruption scheme. Patricia was just the young clerk who processed what her supervisor told her to process."

I felt the pieces of our investigation shifting dramatically, like a kaleidoscope creating an entirely new picture. "So Linda was going to help Patricia expose the person who'd really been behind the corruption? What the heck? She was a blackmailer, but she had limits?"

"That's what her preparation notes suggest. She'd written that Patricia deserved to know the full scope of what she'd been forced to participate in, and that Alderbrite should finally face consequences for what he'd stolen from the community." Derek rubbed his eyes, the exhaustion of his all-night research session clearly catching up with him.

Jet rubbed his temples, looking as confused as I felt. "So if Linda wasn't planning to blackmail the mayor, then Mayor Hendricks didn't have a motive to kill her."

"Unless Patricia didn't know Linda's actual intentions," I said, grasping for some way to salvage our theory. "Maybe Patricia thought she was going to be blackmailed and killed Linda to prevent it, not realizing Linda was trying to help her?"

Derek was already shaking his head and clicking through more files. "That's what I spent most of the night trying to determine," he said, stifling a yawn that reminded me he'd gotten even less sleep than I had. "Linda's investigation went far beyond what any of us understood. She wasn't just looking at historical corruption or individual blackmail opportunities. She was documenting an ongoing criminal operation."

"What kind of ongoing operation?" Kashvi asked, her pen poised over her notebook.

Derek pulled up a complex spreadsheet that looked like it had taken hours to compile. "Linda had connected the original Alderbrite-era corruption to current irregularities in city contracts. She thought the same fraud was happening again, just with different people and more sophisticated methods."

"Current corruption?" I asked. "You mean someone's actively stealing from the city right now?"

"That's what Linda's research suggests. She'd identified several recent contracts that showed the exact same patterns as the Alderbrite schemes—projects with dramatically inflated costs, questionable change orders that doubled original budgets, payments to companies that didn't seem to perform much actual work."

Alistair paused in his coffee service, looking genuinely distressed for the first time since we'd started this investigation. "And whoever's behind the current corruption would have an extremely compelling motive to stop Linda from exposing both the historical scheme and their current operation."

"Yes," Derek said, accepting his coffee refill with obvious gratitude. "Especially if Linda was planning to give all her evidence to Mayor Hendricks, who would be legally and ethically obligated to report it to law enforcement and probably the state attorney general."

I sipped my coffee and tried to process the implications of what Derek had discovered. "So Linda wasn't killed by someone afraid of being exposed for old crimes. She was killed by someone who's actively committing new ones."

"Someone who knew about her scheduled meeting with the mayor and realized that meeting would destroy their current operation," Jet added, settling more deeply into his chair as if we were discussing something far less dangerous than ongoing municipal corruption and murder.

"But who has access to current city contracts and the ability to manipulate them the same way Alderbrite did twenty years ago?" Kashvi asked, her methodical approach making the overwhelming complexity seem slightly more manageable.

Derek's expression was grim, but I could see relief mixed with the fresh worry. At least we weren't planning to accuse an innocent reform-minded mayor of murder. "That's what we need to figure out before we talk to the police. Because if we're right about this, we're dealing with someone who's currently in a position of municipal power and has already demonstrated they're willing to kill to protect their criminal operation."

As I sat in Alistair's overly ornate living room—surrounded by evidence of Linda's far more complex investigation than we'd ever imagined and drinking what was admittedly excellent coffee—I realized we weren't just solving a murder anymore. We were uncovering an active criminal enterprise that had gotten Linda killed, and that might put all of us in danger if we weren't extremely careful about our next steps.

Yesterday's celebration, where I'd watched Mayor Hendricks give passionate speeches about justice and redemption, suddenly felt like it had happened in a different lifetime. She might be innocent of murder, but someone in Nueva Vida's current city government was definitely guilty of both ongoing corruption and killing to cover it up. And Derek didn't know who it was.

"So who do we investigate now?" I asked, the question feeling heavier than it should have.

"Someone with current access to city contracts," Derek said. "Someone who would know about Linda's meeting with the mayor, and someone who could poison her food at the retreat."

"That's a much smaller list than our previous suspects," Kashvi said. "But a much more dangerous one."

"We need to talk to Mayor Hendricks," I said. "She could be involved in the new crime, or just turning a blind eye. We can't just cross her off the list. I don't think we need to get involved with anything beyond clearing Derek's name." That would come with the arrest of the murderer. "Let's try to remember we aren't a band of superheroes out to fight for justice."

20

After leaving Alistair's house on Tuesday morning with our understanding of the case completely transformed, we'd agreed that we needed more time to process Derek's revelations before approaching the police. The discovery that Mayor Hendricks might be innocent while someone else was stealing from the city had turned our entire investigation upside down, and rushing into accusations against unknown corrupt officials seemed like a recipe for disaster. And I couldn't quite put aside a feeling that we were jumping at slim facts to avoid thinking Mayor Hendricks was a criminal.

I was back at EB Eats for the lunch rush, grateful for the familiar rhythm of taking orders and watching Jacquie work her magic on the grill. There's something comforting about the predictable chaos of a busy restaurant—the sizzle of onions hitting hot oil, the cheerful clatter of dishes, the way regular customers settle into their usual spots with no need to be seated.

"You look like you've got something heavy on your mind," Jacquie observed during a brief lull, glancing up from the green chili stew she was stirring with her usual methodical precision.

"This case is way more complicated than we thought," I admitted, refilling the napkin dispensers. "We keep thinking we've figured it out, and then we discover we've been looking at everything completely wrong."

"Well," Jacquie said, "sometimes the best thing you can do is step back and let your brain work on the problem while your hands stay busy with familiar tasks. Solutions have a way of sneaking up on you when you're not trying so hard to force them."

She was right, but it was hard to focus on mundane tasks like napkin dispensers and coffee refills when somewhere in Nueva Vida, a killer was walking around free while Derek remained under suspicion for a crime he didn't commit. And that person could be the mayor despite what we found in the files.

Around two o'clock, when the lunch crowd had thinned to a few lingering customers nursing their coffee and catching up on local gossip, George walked through the door. He looked tired, and I wondered if the official police work had uncovered some of the same disturbing information Derek had found in his late-night research sessions. Should I just lay it all out for him and let the authorities take the load?

"Afternoon, Eliza," he said, settling onto his usual stool at the counter. "Coffee and whatever smells that good coming from the kitchen?"

"Today's special—grilled cheese with tuna and a side of Jacquie's famous coleslaw," I said, pouring him a steaming cup and noting the way his shoulders seemed to relax in the warm atmosphere of the diner. "Jacquie's been tweaking the seasoning all morning, and I think she's finally got it perfect."

"I'll take it," George said, wrapping his hands around the coffee mug like he was trying to absorb its warmth. "I wanted to talk to you about something. Off the record, if that's possible."

I glanced around the nearly empty diner, then leaned against the counter in what I hoped was a casual posture. "What's on your mind?"

"We've been digging deeper into Linda Ramos's background and activities, and we're finding some things that don't match the picture everyone in Nueva Vida has of her," George's voice was careful and measured, as if he was filtering every word to stay professional. "I'm wondering if your amateur investigation has turned up anything similar."

I felt my pulse quicken, recognizing dangerous ground when I stepped on it. This felt like a moment where sharing too much information could put our entire team in jeopardy, but withholding everything might miss an opportunity to help Derek. And could break this unofficial partnership. "What kind of things are we talking about?"

"The kind that suggest Linda might have been involved in activities that weren't as altruistic and community-minded as people believed," George said, taking a sip of his coffee while studying my face over the rim with cop eyes. "Activities that might have given someone a very compelling reason to want her permanently stopped."

"You mean the blackmail operation," I whispered, making a calculated decision to be at least partially honest with him.

George's eyebrows rose in surprise. "So you know about that part of her activities."

"We found evidence that Linda was manipulating

people into providing services for what she claimed were community projects. Free medical care from Dr. Zhang, free retreat weekends from Serenity, access to customer financial information from Emily." I paused, realizing I needed to choose my words carefully, just like he did. "But we also found evidence that she might have been planning something much bigger and more dangerous."

"Bigger in what way?"

I hesitated, then decided that George deserved to know at least part of what we'd discovered, especially if it might help Derek. "George, we think Linda was investigating systematic corruption at city hall. Not just documenting local history, but planning to expose ongoing criminal activity."

George set down his coffee cup with deliberate care, his expression shifting from curious to deeply concerned. "That's an extremely serious accusation, Eliza. And I sincerely hope Derek didn't do anything illegal to uncover this information, because if evidence was obtained through unauthorized access to city systems, it could compromise our entire case against the real perpetrator."

"Derek was very careful about staying within legal boundaries," I said, though inwardly I was hoping his computer skills had been as untraceable as he'd claimed. "He's not stupid enough to jeopardize his own freedom."

"Denise has a point. Amateur investigations are dangerous precisely because they can cross legal lines without realizing it," George said, his voice carrying a warning edge that made me nervous. "You're dealing with powerful people who have enormous amounts to lose, and that makes them unpredictable. You are withholding information from the police—from me."

"We understand the risks," I said, trying to sound more confident than I felt while plating George's sandwich.

George studied my face as if he thought he'd read my mind. "I doubt it, because I really don't want to be investigating your murder next, Eliza. Or Derek's, or anyone else's."

The bell over the door chimed as the Hendersons came in for their usual late lunch, and I waved them toward their favorite booth near the window while continuing our conversation in even lower tones.

"We're not approaching this lightly," I said, delivering George's sandwich. Lola took care of the Hendersons, so I had no excuse to walk away. "But Derek deserves to have his name cleared, and Linda deserves justice, no matter what she did."

"I understand that motivation," George said, biting into his sandwich and inhaling the melted cheese and tuna combination. He chewed and swallowed before continuing. "But formal investigations have legal protections that amateur detective work doesn't have. If you've uncovered evidence of corruption, the safest approach is to turn everything over to law enforcement immediately."

I glanced toward the kitchen, where Jacquie was listening while pretending to organize her spice collection. "Derek found evidence that Linda had been researching city contracts going back twenty years. She'd identified patterns of financial irregularities that suggested systematic fraud. We didn't tell you because it wasn't firm enough for you to act on."

He took another bite; it kind of felt like that interrogation technique where he leaves gaps for me to fill with confessions. When I didn't start talking, he asked, "What kind of patterns specifically?"

"Inflated project costs, questionable change orders that

doubled original budgets, payments to companies that didn't seem to perform much actual work," I said, keeping my voice low and professional. "The same activities from the early 2000s happening again with current contracts."

George was quiet for a long moment, finishing his sandwich while processing what I'd told him. "And you believe Linda was murdered to prevent her from exposing someone?"

"We think Linda was killed to prevent her from giving all her evidence to Mayor Hendricks," I said. "She had an appointment scheduled with the mayor for the Monday after she died. We believe she was planning to turn over everything she'd discovered about both historical and current corruption."

He wiped his hands and took a sip of water. "Why Mayor Hendricks specifically?"

"Because Linda had figured out that Mayor Hendricks was a victim of the original corruption scheme twenty years ago, not a participant." I observed George's face for signs of surprise or confirmation. "She was a junior clerk who tried to report the irregularities and was silenced by her corrupt supervisors."

George rubbed his temples in a gesture I was learning meant he was processing information that aligned with things he already knew but couldn't discuss. "Do you have any theories about who the current corruption involves?"

"That's what Derek's still trying to determine. But whoever it is has current access to city contracts and the power to manipulate them the same way the corruption worked twenty years ago." I paused, studying George's reaction. "How much of this did you already know or suspect?"

"Enough to be very concerned about your safety," he said, finishing his slaw and pushing the plate away. "If you're right about ongoing corruption, you're investigating people with substantial power, significant resources, and a demonstrated willingness to kill to protect their criminal operation."

The bell chimed again as Vic Simons walked in, still in his firefighter uniform and looking like he'd just finished responding to a call. He spotted George and me at the counter and made his way over, his usual easy smile dimming slightly when he noticed the serious atmosphere of our conversation.

"Afternoon," he said, sliding onto the stool next to George. "Hope I'm not interrupting anything important."

"Just discussing the ongoing investigation," George said with professional courtesy that didn't hide his irritation at the interruption.

Vic's expression grew somber. "Any significant progress? The whole situation has everyone in town on edge. People are starting to wonder if Derek really committed murder, or if there's someone else dangerous still walking around Nueva Vida."

"We're exploring all possibilities and following every lead," George said in his diplomatic way that revealed nothing while sounding cooperative.

I poured Vic a cup of coffee, trying to ease the sudden tension that always seemed to develop when these two ended up in the same space. Their professional rivalry was usually more subtle, but the stress of the investigation seemed to bring underlying conflicts to the surface. And I guess me dating both of them didn't help them become friends.

"You know, Eliza" Vic said, "remember when we had dinner at Uncle Brad's place last week? He mentioned something that might be relevant to your investigation."

George's expression darkened at the casual reference to their dinner date, and I could feel the temperature at the counter drop several degrees.

"Brad said Linda Ramos had been asking him detailed questions about some of the construction projects he'd worked on over the years," Vic continued, either oblivious to or ignoring George's obvious irritation—or enjoying it. "Technical questions about costs, timelines, that sort of thing."

George leaned forward with renewed professional interest, setting aside his personal feelings. "Why would she come to him?"

"His background in construction, and he's a friend. She wanted to know whether certain municipal projects seemed overpriced for the work involved, or if he'd noticed any patterns in which companies got awarded city contracts, whether he'd ever seen evidence of substandard work being passed off as meeting specifications." Vic shook his head while I automatically refilled George's coffee cup. "Brad said Linda seemed to know more about Nueva Vida's business dealings than someone doing casual research should reasonably know."

I exchanged glances with George while he processed this new information. It confirmed what Derek had discovered about Linda's investigation. Did it add to George's?

"Did Brad tell anyone else about Linda's visit and her unusual questions?" George asked, his professional instincts overriding his personal feelings about Vic.

"He mentioned it to several people at the hardware store, and probably to some of his regular coffee companions at the café." Vic grinned with the easy humor that made him so popular in town. "You know how Uncle Brad is

—he doesn't keep much to himself, especially when someone asks him interesting questions about his work."

That information was both reassuring and concerning. Reassuring because it meant Linda's corruption investigation wasn't a closely guarded secret that only the killer had known about. Concerning because it meant dangerous information about ongoing criminal activity was circulating through Nueva Vida's efficient gossip network, possibly alerting the real perpetrators.

"Vic," George said, "if your uncle remembers anything else specific about his conversation with Linda, would you have him call me at the station? And please ask him not to discuss this with anyone else—we don't need to put more civilians in potential danger."

"Of course," Vic said. "Hey, should I be worried about Uncle Brad's safety? If someone killed Linda to stop her investigation..."

"Just have him be careful about who he talks to and what he says," George advised. "And if he remembers anything that seemed significant about Linda's questions, he should call me, not Eliza."

After both George and Vic left, I took a break in the alley where we'd put a small table and two chairs. Alone with my thoughts and the familiar end-of-afternoon routine of cleaning and restocking, I tried to sort out everything. The case, which kept twisting and turning, and my love life. Did I need to choose? George was interesting when off duty, but that was rare and he kept trying to stop me investigating. Vic was easygoing and charming and never tried to keep me safe.

I couldn't let romance pull me off the important topic. How to solve the case.

The conversation had clarified some things while

making others more complex. George clearly knew more about Linda's activities than he was saying, but he was also concerned about our safety. The fact that Linda's interest in city contracts was public knowledge was both good and bad —good because it meant we weren't the only ones who'd figured out part of her investigation, bad because we might not be the only ones in danger. Did Patricia know the gossip?

21

The Tuesday evening meeting at Alistair's felt like a final strategy session before battle. Derek had arrived with two large pizzas from Lorenzo's—one pepperoni, one vegetarian—and I was relieved to see him looking less pale and exhausted than he had during our morning revelations about Mayor Hendricks possibly being innocent of murder. Getting away from his computer screen and the weight of constantly analyzing evidence had clearly done him some good.

"I figured we'd need fuel for this conversation," Derek said, opening the pizza boxes on Alistair's mahogany dining room table. "This is going to be complicated."

Alistair had outdone himself with the evening setup—proper china plates for the pizza, linen napkins, and what appeared to be his best crystal glasses for the wine Kashvi had thoughtfully contributed. I realized how different he was in his own home compared to his—let's say lack of ambition at Dunes, where he'd been serving the same reliable but uninspired menu for decades with minimal fuss. Here, he approached hospitality as if it was performance art.

"If we're going to plan a confrontation about murder and corruption," he announced with typical dramatic flair, "we should do it with proper style and adequate refreshment."

"So," I said, accepting a slice of the vegetarian pizza, "we've established that Mayor Hendricks was caught up in corruption twenty years ago but was probably a victim rather than a perpetrator. We know Linda was planning to meet with her to expose the real criminals, or to blackmail her. George knows most of it, but I didn't get the feeling he was rushing off to make an arrest."

Derek pointed at a sheet of paper with bullet points on it, balancing a slice of pepperoni pizza in his other hand. "We have Linda's files showing she was investigating systematic corruption going back decades. We have evidence of the original scheme and documentation of current irregularities that suggest the same criminal pattern is happening again. A copy of a complaint from Patricia about the inconsistencies. But that could have been a cover, right? To make it look like she wasn't involved."

"We don't have proof that she killed Linda," Jet said, reaching for his wineglass and settling back in his chair. "Of course we also don't have proof she didn't. Just evidence that someone involved in current corruption would have compelling motives."

Kashvi paused to wipe her fingers on one of Alistair's expensive cloth napkins. "What exactly are we hoping to accomplish with a confrontation? Get someone to confess spontaneously? And, really, why are we having so much trouble taking the next step?"

"Because it's the mayor. If we get it wrong, there will be huge repercussions. I already shared most of our corruption findings with George at the diner this afternoon," I admitted, feeling heat rise in my cheeks as I anticipated their reactions. "I told him about Linda's investigation into municipal contracts, about her planned meeting with Mayor Hendricks, about the evidence of ongoing criminal activity."

Alistair nearly choked on his wine, setting down his crystal glass with enough force to make me wince. "You did what? Eliza, the police will take forever to assemble proper warrants and navigate all the bureaucratic procedures! By the time they're ready to move, whoever's behind this could destroy evidence, flee the jurisdiction, or eliminate anyone who knows too much about their operation!" He was warming to his dramatic theme now, gesturing expansively with his pizza slice. "We need to confront the responsible parties ourselves, tonight, before they realize the investigative net is closing in! The authorities are too slow!"

"Alistair," I said, cutting through his theatrical enthusiasm, "we are absolutely not going to storm city hall like some kind of amateur vigilante gang. That's how people get hurt or arrested."

"Then what do you suggest?" Derek asked, his voice carrying the weight of the suspicion he'd been under for over a week. "Because if someone in city government killed Linda to protect their corruption scheme, they're not going to hesitate to eliminate other potential threats to their operation."

I reached for another slice of pizza, using the familiar action of eating to help me think through our limited and dangerous options. Sometimes, the physical act of consuming good food helped me focus, even when I wasn't particularly hungry. "We need to approach this with a clear plan. I think we're stuck because we don't want to believe there's this much corruption in Nueva Vida. We need to pick a theory and act on it."

"Well, we should. I mean the old sheriff is in jail, right?

What do you mean a clear plan?" Kashvi asked, picking the cheese off her crust.

"We know Linda was investigating both past and current corruption. We know she was planning to give her evidence to Mayor Hendricks, who would have been obligated to report it to law enforcement. Someone with current access to city contracts would have known about that meeting and understood what it meant for their criminal operation." I set down my pizza slice as the plan formed. "What if we approached Mayor Hendricks directly and explained what we've discovered? Choose the option that she's just an innocent bystander."

Derek nodded, understanding dawning on his face. "If she's innocent of murder, she'll want to cooperate with exposing the real corruption and clearing both her name and mine."

"And if she's somehow involved in the current criminal activity," Jet added, "her reaction will tell us everything we need to know about her guilt or innocence. That's risky, but I'll give it a shot."

"I have a relationship with her," I said, not willing to let Derek take the risk.

"Eliza is right, Derek. She'd done this before as well." Alistair was pacing now, gesturing with his empty wine glass. "That's a much more civilized approach than my vigilante committee idea! You go in appearing to offer assistance and information, and observe her response! I approve!"

"It's still dangerous," Derek said, his expression troubled. "If she's involved in current corruption or if she killed Linda to protect historical secrets, approaching her could put Eliza in serious jeopardy. I'm the one who's facing a charge already."

"But I'm our best chance to get answers without waiting

for official police procedures," I argued, though I was feeling the weight of what I was proposing. "I can say I want to talk about the gang project. Then, when I'm in her office, I'll tell her what we have. If she's innocent, she'll be grateful for the warning and eager to cooperate with exposing the real criminals. If she's guilty, she might reveal something that gives us the proof we need."

"I still don't like the idea of you going in alone to confront someone who might be a murderer," Kashvi said. "Not just you, Eliza, anyone."

"She doesn't need to be alone," Jet said. "We could position ourselves nearby—maybe in the city hall parking area or the coffee shop across the street. Close enough to call for help immediately if things go wrong, but not so close that we interfere with getting an honest reaction."

"Do we really have enough evidence to justify putting Eliza in this position?" Derek asked, stacking his research papers. "I mean, are we confident enough in our theories to risk someone's safety? If we think there's a strong possibility the mayor is guilty, that's too much danger."

I thought about Derek still living under the cloud of murder suspicion, about Linda's complex legacy of both helping and manipulating people, about a community that deserved to know the truth about corruption in their local government.

"We don't have enough concrete evidence for George to make immediate arrests," I said, working through my reasoning out loud. "But we have enough circumstantial evidence and logical connections to know that someone needs to ask Mayor Hendricks some direct, challenging questions about Linda's death and her own involvement in municipal corruption. The police can't do that because she'll ask for a lawyer either way."

"And if she's innocent of murder? And you expose this conspiracy?" Alistair asked, with obvious reluctance to abandon his fantasies of dramatic confrontations.

"Then hopefully our questions will help her understand the real danger she's in from whoever killed Linda," I said. "And maybe she'll have information that helps us identify the actual killer."

"And if she's guilty?" Derek asked.

"Then hopefully she'll realize that her position is hopeless and confess before anyone else gets hurt," I said, though I wasn't convinced by my own optimistic reasoning.

Derek closed his laptop with finality, looking deeply troubled by what we were planning. "Are we absolutely sure this is the right approach? Going around the official police investigation to confront a sitting mayor?"

"George has access to official resources and legal procedures that we don't have," I said. "We're just... following up on legitimate community concerns about municipal corruption and its connection to Linda's death."

As we gathered our belongings and prepared to leave Alistair's house—which had served as our investigation headquarters for over a week now—I found myself second-guessing the confrontation plan I'd just convinced everyone to support. What if I was completely wrong about Patricia's involvement? What if approaching her just made the entire situation worse for Derek and more dangerous for all of us?

But then I thought about the former gang members who'd found genuine hope through Patricia's support of the gang program, about a community that had placed their trust in both Linda's volunteer work and Patricia's political leadership, about Derek's quiet dignity and patience in the face of false accusations that were destroying his reputation and his freedom.

If Patricia Hendricks was innocent of murder, she deserved the opportunity to clear her name and help expose the real criminals. If she was guilty, she needed to face the consequences of her actions before she could hurt anyone else.

22

Wednesday morning arrived with a crisp clarity that New Mexico fall days sometimes bring, but I felt anything but clear-headed as I walked toward city hall for what we all knew would be the ultimate confrontation. My stomach was churning with a mixture of nerves and the three cups of coffee I'd consumed while getting ready, trying to fuel my courage for what might be the most dangerous conversation of my life.

Kashvi and Jet were already in position according to our carefully planned strategy—Kashvi in the reception area with a stack of business permit applications, pretending to research requirements for expanding the bookstore, and Jet examining the historical photographs in the hallway like a tourist interested in Nueva Vida's municipal history. I'd called Kashvi's phone before entering the building and left the line open, my device tucked into my jacket pocket where it wouldn't be obvious but could pick up our conversation for evidence—we'd tested it earlier.

The city hall building was a modest adobe structure that perfectly fit Nueva Vida's small-town character, with pottery planters flanking the entrance and hand-painted signs directing visitors to various municipal departments. The morning bustle of civic business—people paying water bills, applying for permits, conducting the routine administrative tasks of community life—provided perfect cover for our investigative plan.

"I was hoping to speak with Mayor Hendricks," I told the receptionist, a cheerful woman in her sixties who probably knew everyone in town by their first name and family history. "I'm Eliza Burton, from EB Eats. It's about an urgent community matter."

I caught Kashvi's eye as she looked up from her permit applications, giving her a subtle nod to confirm everything was proceeding according to plan. Jet stood near the hallway entrance, studying a black-and-white photograph of Nueva Vida's first mining operation with convincing academic interest.

"Oh, of course! You're the one who spoke so beautifully at the gang resolution meeting last week," the receptionist said with obvious enthusiasm, reaching for her phone. "Mayor Hendricks will be delighted to see you even without an appointment. She's been so proud of how that program turned out... Mayor? Eliza Burton is here to see you about a community matter... Yes, I'll send her right back."

The mayor's office was at the end of a short hallway lined with framed photographs documenting Nueva Vida's civic history—the founding of the town, celebrations and festivals spanning decades, ribbon cuttings and community achievements that represented the local pride Patricia Hendricks had spent her career cultivating. As I passed Jet, he was leaning in to read a brass plaque about municipal incorporation, positioned close enough to the mayor's office that he'd hear clearly if anything went seriously wrong.

Mayor Hendricks' door was open, and she rose from behind her desk as I approached, her smile warm and genuine making what we were planning feel even more morally complex. She was wearing a navy suit that projected professional competence while remaining approachable—the perfect outfit for a popular small-town mayor.

"Eliza! What a wonderful surprise on a busy Wednesday morning. Please, come in and make yourself comfortable," she said, gesturing to a cushioned chair across from her desk, which was covered with neat stacks of papers and what appeared to be budget reports. She left the door open, which was perfect for maintaining the illusion of a casual community conversation while ensuring Jet could overhear if our discussion took a dangerous turn. "Can I offer you coffee? I just made a fresh pot, and it's quite good for municipal building coffee."

The office was decorated with thoughtful care, local artwork featuring Nueva Vida landscapes, plants that were well-tended and thriving, a bookshelf lined with volumes on public administration, community development, and several books about restorative justice principles. It felt like the workspace of someone who cared about doing effective, ethical work for her constituents.

"Coffee would be wonderful," I said, accepting the mug she offered with hands that I was glad to see weren't trembling. The china was simple but elegant, and the coffee was indeed excellent—rich, perfectly brewed.

"I'm always happy to meet with community members, especially those who've been so supportive of our innovative programs," she said, settling back behind her desk with expectant friendliness. "What's on your mind this morning?"

I took a sip of coffee, using the moment to gather both

my thoughts and my courage. "It's about Linda Ramos and the research she'd been conducting into city business and historical contracts. I wanted to give you a heads-up that her name has come up in some rather concerning contexts during our investigation."

The change in Mayor Hendricks' expression was subtle but unmistakable—a slight tightening around her eyes, a barely perceptible stiffening of her posture, the way her coffee cup paused halfway to her lips before she set it down with deliberate care.

"I'm not sure I follow what you mean," she said, her voice maintaining its pleasant tone while her body language shifted to something more guarded. "What kind of research are you referring to?"

"Linda had been researching old city contracts, particularly from the early 2000s period. She seemed especially interested in payment processing procedures and administrative oversight from that time." I watched her face as I delivered the crucial information. "Your name came up repeatedly in her research notes as someone who'd worked in that department during the relevant time period."

Mayor Hendricks set down her coffee cup. I could see her mind working behind her careful political mask. "Many people worked in various city administration roles over the years, Eliza. It wouldn't be unusual for a researcher to contact former employees about past procedures and policies."

She stood up smoothly and walked to her office door, closing it with a soft click that seemed to echo in the suddenly smaller, more isolated space. The casual friendliness had evaporated from her demeanor, replaced by something more calculating and cautious.

My heart sank as I realized Jet could no longer hear our

conversation, and I resisted the urge to check whether my phone was still transmitting to Kashvi. The office felt much warmer and more enclosed, and I could smell the faint scent of the mayor's expensive perfume mixing with the coffee aroma and the slight mustiness of old building ventilation.

"The thing is," I continued as gently as possible, "Linda wasn't conducting casual historical research. She'd discovered some significant irregularities in those old municipal contracts, and she seemed to believe that people should be held accountable for what she'd uncovered, even after all these years."

"Accountable in what way?" The question came out sharper and more defensive than she'd probably intended, and I saw her catch herself, softening her tone to something more diplomatically appropriate. "I mean, if there were minor administrative errors or oversights from decades ago, the statute of limitations would apply to any potential legal issues."

"Unless the same problems were still happening," I said, playing the card Derek had discovered. "Linda seemed to think she'd identified ongoing patterns of corruption, current irregularities that suggested the same criminal schemes were continuing with different people."

Mayor Hendricks was silent for a long moment, staring at her coffee cup as if it contained answers to impossible questions. When she finally looked up, her expression had transformed—someone wary had replaced the warm, approachable community leader, calculating, and desperate.

"Eliza, why are you here in my office?" she asked, dropping any pretense of casual conversation. "If you have legitimate concerns about current city administration, there are established proper channels for reporting them. Citizens don't just walk into the mayor's office making vague accusations about financial irregularities."

"I'm here because Linda had an appointment scheduled with you for the Monday after she died," I said, playing what I knew was my biggest and most dangerous card. "And because Derek McKay is still under suspicion for a murder I'm absolutely certain he didn't commit."

The silence stretched between us, filled only by the muffled sounds of normal city hall business continuing beyond the closed door—phones ringing in distant offices, footsteps echoing in hallways, the steady hum of air conditioning and municipal life. Mayor Hendricks picked up an expensive pen from her desk and began turning it nervously between her fingers, a small gesture that seemed at odds with her usual composed public persona.

"What exactly do you think you know about that scheduled appointment?" she asked, her voice carefully controlled.

"I think Linda was planning to confront you about the corruption from twenty years ago," I said, delivering what I hoped sounded like a confident accusation. The way she'd reacted told me our mayor wasn't innocent of anything. "I think she'd found concrete evidence that implicated you in financial irregularities, and she was going to use that information to pressure or control you somehow."

Mayor Hendricks' laugh was brittle and without humor, a sound that sent chills down my spine. "And you think I killed her to prevent that conversation from happening?"

"I think Linda Ramos had an exceptional talent for finding people's deepest vulnerabilities and using them for her own purposes," I said, trying to maintain eye contact while my heart hammered against my ribs. "And I think you might have felt like you had no choice but to stop her permanently."

She was quiet again, turning to stare out the window at the street where normal Nueva Vida life was continuing—people walking to work, cars navigating the modest downtown traffic, children waiting for school buses, the comfortable rhythm of a small town going about its daily business completely unaware of the confrontation happening in their mayor's office.

"You have no idea what it's like," she said finally, her voice barely above a whisper but carrying more emotion than I'd ever heard from her. "To spend twenty years building something good, helping people, making a real difference in your community, only to have someone threaten to destroy it all over mistakes you made when you were barely out of college and trying to do your best."

My heart sank as I realized what she was admitting—the confession I'd been hoping for and dreading in equal measure. "Patricia..."

"I was twenty-three years old when I started working for the city," she continued, as if she hadn't heard me speak her name. "Completely inexperienced, trying to do a good job and make my supervisors happy. When Jeb Alderbrite told me to process those inflated payments, to approve those questionable change orders without asking questions, I thought he knew what he was doing. I thought I was being a cooperative team player."

"But you tried to report the irregularities," I said, remembering Derek's research. "We found records of your complaints, your attempts to do the right thing."

"Much good it did me or anyone else." Her smile was bitter and filled with old pain. "Jeb told me I was overstepping my authority, that questioning his administrative decisions could cost me my job and destroy my future in public service. So I kept quiet and did what I was told, like a good little clerk. And yes, some of that stolen money eventually found its way into my first campaign fund, though I told myself it was legitimate donations from grateful contractors."

She turned back to face me, and I could see twenty years of guilt and rationalizing warring in her expression. "I've spent every single day since then trying to make up for those choices, Eliza. Every community program I've supported, every progressive initiative I've championed, every dollar I've saved the taxpayers—it was all my way of paying back what was taken, of proving I deserved the trust people placed in me."

"Linda didn't understand that you were trying to make amends," I said, hoping to keep her talking while Kashvi called for help.

"Linda Ramos was a predator who used people's shame to control them," Mayor Hendricks said, her voice hardening with years of buried resentment. "She discovered my past mistakes and saw an opportunity to control me forever. She wanted me to look the other way while she expanded her blackmail operation, to use my position to protect her network of victims and informants."

"So you killed her," I said, the words hanging in the air between us like a physical presence.

The mayor stared at me for a long moment, and I could see her weighing her options, calculating whether denial was still possible or if the truth was her only remaining strategy.

"I met her at the retreat that Saturday morning," she said finally, her voice taking on the flat tone of someone recounting events she'd replayed countless times. "I told the staff I was there to discuss charity fair permits and facility usage for the school, but I wanted to confront Linda about what she was planning to say to me during our scheduled Monday meeting."

"What happened during that confrontation?"

"She laid it all out for me with complete confidence that she had me trapped and helpless." Mayor Hendricks' voice grew bitter. "How she knew about the old corruption, how she could destroy my career with a single anonymous phone call to the state attorney general. But she was graciously willing to keep quiet if I helped her expand her operation; if I used my municipal influence to protect her network of informants and blackmail victims."

The mayor walked back to the window, her silhouette framed against the morning light. "Linda called it a partnership for community improvement. She'd provide intelligence about residents who might need what she called guidance toward better behavior, and I'd make sure no one in law enforcement or city administration looked too closely at her methods. All for the greater good of Nueva Vida, of course."

I tried to process what she was revealing. We'd been completely wrong about Linda's intentions—she hadn't been planning to help the mayor expose corruption, she'd been trying to recruit her into an expanded blackmail enterprise. She didn't care that Patricia wasn't in on the original crime.

"And when you refused her offer?"

"I told her I'd rather confess my own crimes than help her hurt more innocent people." Mayor Hendricks turned back to face me, and I could see tears gathering in her eyes. "And Linda laughed at me. She said no one would believe I'd been an unwilling participant, that twenty years of good work wouldn't matter once the corruption allegations became public. She said I'd go to federal prison as an accomplice while she walked away free as a community-minded whistle-blower."

I felt sick to my stomach, but I knew I had to keep her talking until help arrived. "So you decided to poison her energy bar?"

"I brought the foxglove extract with me to the retreat, thinking I might need some kind of leverage of my own," she said, her voice shifting from calculated control to something more broken and filled with regret. "When Linda stepped away to use the restroom during our conversation, I mixed the extract into the almond butter on her snack. I didn't much care when she ate it."

Her voice cracked. "I told myself I was protecting the community from a dangerous predator who was manipulating vulnerable people. But really, I was just protecting myself and everything I'd built from the consequences of choices I'd made twenty years ago."

"Patricia," I said as gently as possible, "it's over now. You need to call Detective Kramer, tell him what happened. If you cooperate and show genuine remorse—"

"Cooperate toward what outcome?" she interrupted, her voice rising with desperate anger. "Maybe they'll give me life in prison instead of the death penalty? Maybe they'll let me serve my sentence in a minimum-security facility?" She shook her head with bitter resignation. "Twenty years of genuine public service, of helping people and improving this community, and this is how my legacy ends."

She moved toward her desk with sudden purpose, and for a hopeful moment I thought she was reaching for the phone to call George and surrender. Instead, she opened the top drawer and pulled out a small revolver that gleamed dully in the office lighting. The sight of the weapon made my blood run cold, and I could hear my heartbeat thundering in my ears loud enough that I was surprised she couldn't hear it too.

I thought I heard footsteps quickening in the hallway—hopefully Jet reacting to the escalating tension he could sense even through the closed door.

"I'm genuinely sorry, Eliza," she said, her voice filled with what sounded like authentic regret. "You seem like a good person, and this community is lucky to have someone who cares as much as you do. But I can't let you destroy everything I've spent twenty years building and protecting."

She paused, glancing toward the closed door with calculation. "Your friends will probably decide it's much safer to keep quiet about their theories after you're gone. People tend to be more cautious when they understand the real stakes involved in challenging powerful people."

My mind raced, trying to understand how she thought she might get away with shooting someone in city hall during business hours. "Patricia, you can't just shoot me in your office. Everyone in the building will hear the gunshot. You'll be caught immediately and investigated."

Her smile was sad but absolutely determined. "I'll tell them you came here making wild, unfounded accusations about corruption, that you became aggressive when I refused to confess to crimes I didn't commit. Self-defense against an unhinged amateur detective who'd become obsessed." She shifted the gun. "Who do you think they'll believe—the respected mayor with twenty years of exemplary public service, or the diner owner who's been playing amateur detective and making desperate accusations?"

The weapon was pointing at me now, and I realized that I had seriously underestimated how desperate and cornered Patricia Hendricks had become. The office air felt thick and oppressive, and I could taste the metallic tang of pure fear in my mouth.

I could only hope that Kashvi had heard enough through the phone connection to call George immediately, and that Jet was close enough to the office to intervene before the mayor decided she had no choice but to pull the trigger and eliminate the final threat to her carefully constructed new life.

24

The gun was steady in Mayor Hendricks' hand, pointing at my chest, when the office door burst open with enough force to rattle the framed photographs documenting Nueva Vida's civic achievements on the walls. Jet filled the doorway, his face pale but determined, clearly terrified but unwilling to let fear stop him from trying to save me.

"Let her go!" he said, his voice shaking despite his obvious attempt to sound authoritative and in control. Behind him, I could hear rapid footsteps echoing in the hallway and Kashvi's voice talking urgently on her phone— calling for immediate police backup as we'd planned.

Mayor Hendricks spun toward the door, the gun wavering between Jet and me as she tried to process this new threat to her desperate plan. "Stay back! This doesn't concern you!"

"Please," Jet said, his hands raised and trembling despite his attempt at calm negotiation, "just put the gun down. We can work this out peacefully."

"There's nothing left to work out," Mayor Hendricks

said, her voice cracking. "It's over. All of it. Twenty years of trying to make up for my mistakes, of helping this community, and it's all going to be destroyed anyway."

"Patricia," I said as calmly as possible, not daring to move from my chair but trying to keep her talking, "you said yourself that you've spent twenty years helping this community. That genuine service matters. People will remember the good you've done."

"Will they?" She laughed bitterly, the gun still moving between us. "When the newspapers write sensational headlines about the mayor who stole taxpayer money—even if it's not true—and committed murder? When they tear apart every program I supported, every initiative I championed? The gang resolution program that we celebrated just yesterday—do you honestly think that survives when people find out it was supported by a killer?"

The mention of the gang program and the kids who'd found hope through it hit me like a physical blow. She was right about the potential damage—all the genuine good work, all the teenagers who'd discovered they could matter in positive ways, would be tainted by association with her crimes. The devastating irony was that someone who authentically believed in second chances had thrown away her own redemption by committing murder.

"Those kids deserve their second chances," I said with as much conviction as I could manage. "And you can still help protect what they've built by doing the right thing now. Put the gun down, talk to George, tell him everything. Show the community that you're still the person who believed in justice and making amends."

From the hallway came the unmistakable sound of more footsteps—heavy boots that meant law enforcement had arrived in response to Kashvi's emergency call. Mayor

Hendricks heard it too, and I saw something shift in her expression, a desperate final calculation taking place behind her eyes.

"They're here," she whispered, and for a hopeful moment the gun drooped in her hand.

"Patricia," Jet said, his voice still unsteady but gaining strength from pure desperation to save lives, "you know this is wrong. Eliza came here to help you, to warn you about the investigation. Don't make everything worse by hurting someone who was trying to be your friend."

The office door opened wider, and George appeared behind Jet, his service weapon drawn but pointed down at the floor, with two uniformed officers positioned right behind him. His face was grim.

"Mayor Hendricks," George said with remarkable calm, "I need you to put the weapon down. You know this situation can't end well if you keep pointing that gun at innocent people."

"There's been a misunderstanding, Detective Kramer," Mayor Hendricks said, her voice taking on the practiced political tone she'd used for decades of public service. "Ms. Burton came here making wild accusations about city administration, became aggressive when I refused to validate her conspiracy theories. I was defending myself against what appeared to be an unhinged attack."

George's expression didn't change, but I could see him processing her attempted explanation with professional skepticism. "A misunderstanding involving a loaded weapon pointed at community members?"

"An unfortunate escalation of what should have been a simple clarification of facts," she said, though her voice was losing its political polish and becoming more desperate with each word.

"Mayor Hendricks," George said, "I've been listening to your conversation through an open phone line. I heard your confession about poisoning Linda Ramos. There's no misunderstanding here."

The political mask cracked completely, and Mayor Hendricks' shoulders sagged with defeat. "You heard everything?"

"Everything," George confirmed. "Including your explanation of how you poisoned her energy bar with foxglove extract, and why you thought killing her was your only option."

"I never meant for any of this to happen," she said, her voice barely audible now. "I just wanted to serve my community honestly, to make up for what I'd done when I was young and stupid. And then Linda showed up with her threats and her schemes, and I panicked."

She looked around the office that had been the center of her political life for so many years—the local artwork, the thriving plants, the books about public service and community development that represented her genuine commitment to good governance.

Slowly, with movements that suggested she understood her options had run out, Mayor Hendricks set the gun on her desk and sank back into her chair. "I never meant to hurt anyone. I just wanted it all to stop."

George holstered his weapon and nodded to one of the uniformed officers, who stepped forward to secure the gun and begin the arrest process. "Mayor Hendricks, I'm placing you under arrest for the murder of Linda Ramos and for threatening Ms. Burton."

As the officer began reading her Miranda rights, Mayor Hendricks looked up at me with something that might have been gratitude mixed with profound regret. "Eliza, I hope the gang program survives this. Those kids deserve their second chances, even if I threw away mine."

"They'll get them," I said, meaning it. "The program works because the principles are sound, not because of who supported it. Will and the tribal council will make sure it continues."

George waited until the formal arrest procedures were complete, then looked at me, Kashvi, and Jet with concern. "You three will need to give detailed statements about everything you heard and witnessed here today, but first I want to make sure everyone's physically and emotionally okay."

"Shaken up but unharmed," I said, realizing I was indeed trembling with delayed reaction to being held at gunpoint. Adrenaline might be a survival trait, but it did a real number on my body. "Jet's quick thinking probably saved my life."

"Kashvi's phone call definitely saved your life," George said. "And this whole confrontation was incredibly dangerous and poorly planned. You're lucky it didn't end much worse."

As the uniformed officers led Mayor Hendricks out of city hall in handcuffs, I saw the shocked faces of city employees and citizens who had gathered in the hallways after hearing the commotion. Some looked bewildered, others appeared heartbroken—people trying to process the reality that their trusted mayor had just been arrested for murder.

The hardest conversations would come later— explaining everything to Will and the gang kids who had trusted in the mayor's belief in second chances, helping them understand that the principles of restorative justice remained valid even when the people who championed them failed to live up to their own ideals.

As we walked out of city hall into the bright New Mexico afternoon, I couldn't help but think that Nueva Vida would need its own kind of community healing now. The truth about both Linda's predatory blackmail operation and Patricia's desperate cover-up murder would shake everyone's faith in the people they'd trusted most.

25

Thursday morning at EB Eats felt like the first genuinely normal day we'd had in over a week. It was a relief to return to the familiar rhythm of morning service after Wednesday's chaos—fielding endless questions from curious customers who wanted every detail about Mayor Hendricks' dramatic arrest at city hall. The coffee was brewing with its usual invigorating aroma, Jacquie was humming while she prepped the grill for the next order, and the familiar sounds of plates clinking and bacon sizzling filled the kitchen like a soundtrack to normalcy.

Derek McKay had been cleared of all charges yesterday afternoon, and the news had spread through Nueva Vida faster than butter melting on hot toast. I'd fielded at least fifty phone calls and twice as many in-person questions from customers who couldn't quite believe their beloved community had harbored both a blackmailer and a murderer.

I was refilling the coffee station when Derek himself walked through the front door, looking better than I'd seen him since this whole nightmare had begun ten days ago. His shoulders were straighter, his color was healthier, and for the first time since his arrest, he was smiling.

"Derek!" I called out, abandoning the coffee station to give him a quick, relieved hug. "How are you feeling this morning?"

"Like I can actually breathe again," he said, accepting the coffee I poured for him with a giant smile. "I wanted to come by and thank you—all of you—for believing in my innocence when it would have been much easier to assume I was guilty and distance yourselves from the scandal."

"We never doubted you for a single second," I said, though that wasn't completely honest. There had been dark moments when even I had wondered if we might be wrong about his character. But that was in the past now.

"Alistair's been telling everyone in town that he was the criminal mastermind behind solving the case," Derek said with a grin that suggested his sense of humor had returned. "He's transformed the entire investigation into this elaborate story where he single-handedly exposed decades of corruption and caught a killer through brilliant deductive reasoning."

I had to laugh, imagining Alistair holding court at Dunes with dramatic versions of events. "Of course he has. How much of the actual story involves the rest of us doing any work?"

"Oh, we get mentioned prominently," Derek said, his eyes twinkling with amusement. "As his capable assistants who followed his brilliant deductions and carried out his strategic plans. According to Alistair's version, he practically solved the entire case from the comfort of his living room while serving excellent tea."

The bell over the door chimed, and George walked in

looking more relaxed and well-rested than I'd seen him in weeks. The dark circles under his eyes were gone, and he smiled broadly when he spotted Derek at the counter.

"Good morning, Derek," George said warmly, settling onto his usual stool. "It's excellent to see you out and about, cleared and free to rebuild your life."

"Feels pretty amazing," Derek admitted, relief brightening his voice. "Though I have to admit, I'm looking forward to getting back to cooking and catering instead of playing amateur detective. I'm thinking of expanding my catering business—maybe hiring some help now that my reputation's been restored."

"That sounds like a wonderful plan," I said, pouring George his usual coffee. "The regular breakfast this morning?"

"Actually, make it the biggest breakfast you've got on the menu," George said with genuine enthusiasm. "I think I can finally enjoy my food again without worrying about murder investigations and corrupt politicians."

As I called his order back to Jacquie, the bell chimed again, and Kashvi and Jet arrived together, both looking pleased with themselves and carrying a small stack of books.

"Perfect timing," Kashvi said. "We just came from the bookstore, and I have some fun news to share."

"What kind of fun?" I asked, though I was already smiling at her expression.

"Mrs. Patterson's book club has officially declared our investigation more engaging and better plotted than any mystery novel they've read all year," Jet said with a grin that suggested he was as entertained by this as the rest of us.

"They want to invite you to speak at their next monthly meeting," Kashvi added, enjoying my horrified expression.

"Something about real-life detective techniques and practical community problem-solving applications."

"Absolutely not," I said, holding up my hands in mock horror. "I am retiring from the amateur detective business. From now on, the biggest mystery in my life is going to be figuring out creative daily specials and whether we should expand our weekend brunch menu."

"Speaking of mysteries," George said with professional curiosity, "what did I order for breakfast?"

"Green chili breakfast burrito with a guacamole, cooked with love. No murder, no crime, nothing but hope life will stay sunny," I said, and everyone laughed.

The morning crowd began filtering in with comforting predictability—Mrs. Waverly with her daily crossword puzzle and just a coffee, dear, order. The Henderson family for their weekly breakfast adventure, a handful of tourists who'd heard about our sourdough pancakes and wanted to experience them for themselves.

Around ten o'clock, Will appeared with Cassidey, both of them looking serious but determined in a way that suggested they had important news to share.

"Eliza," Will said, approaching the counter, "we wanted to update you on the gang resolution program's future. The tribal council met over the weekend to discuss how to continue, even if city hall didn't want to support it, and they've asked me to coordinate the program going forward."

"That's wonderful," I said, meaning it. "You're the perfect person for that role. Those kids trust you, and you understand what they're going through."

"They want to continue with their community service projects," Cassidey added, her voice carrying maturity that continued to surprise me. "Eddie said they've been talking about starting a peer mentorship program for younger kids who might be heading down the wrong path."

"It's like Mayor Hendricks always said," Will continued, "second chances work when people believe in them and are willing to do the hard work. The kids don't want her mistakes and crimes to undo all the progress they've made."

I felt a warm glow of pride hearing about the program's survival and growth. Despite everything that had happened —the murder, the corruption, the betrayal of trust—the principles of restorative justice and community healing were strong enough to survive the scandal and continue helping people.

"Any word on what's happening with city government leadership?" Jet asked, settling in with his coffee.

"Rebecca Torres, the current city manager, is stepping up as acting mayor until the special election can be organized," George said, pleased with this development. "She's promised a comprehensive audit of all city contracts and financial procedures. Apparently, she's been wanting to clean house for several years but never had the political support to challenge entrenched practices."

"And the broader corruption investigation?" I asked, refilling George's coffee cup.

"That's still ongoing and will probably take months to unravel," George said, switching to his professional voice. "We're still working to identify who restarted the corruption scheme, because Mayor Hendricks was clearly a victim of the original operation, not the current perpetrator. The encouraging news is that most of the stolen money from both schemes can be tracked and recovered. Ironically, Patricia kept meticulous financial records, probably because she was planning to pay back what she'd been forced to take."

Derek finished his coffee and stood up, pulling out his wallet. "I should get going. I have three catering jobs scheduled for this week—word's gotten out that I'm innocent and business is picking up faster than I expected."

"Derek," I said as he headed toward the door, struck by a sudden idea, "wait a minute. You mentioned you're thinking of hiring help for your expanding catering business?"

"Yeah, the demand is increasing faster than I can handle alone, especially with larger events. I'll need someone reliable soon." He paused, looking curious. "Why do you ask?"

I glanced toward the kitchen where Anthone was working on lunch prep, then back to Derek with a mixture of excitement and maternal worry. "Would you be interested in talking to Anthone about the position? He's got genuine culinary talent, and he's been wanting to expand his experience beyond diner cooking into more creative food service."

Derek's face lit up with interest and possibility. "That's a brilliant idea. I could use someone who already understands kitchen work flow and has good instincts about food preparation and presentation."

"It would mean I'd have to find a replacement cook here at the diner," I said, the words coming out before I could second-guess the generous impulse. "But Anthone deserves the opportunity to grow his skills and explore his potential, and I think you two would work exceptionally well together."

"Let me talk to him right now," Derek said, his excitement clear. "If he's interested and available, we could start with some weekend catering jobs, see how the partnership develops."

"Anthone," I called toward the kitchen, feeling a familiar mix of pride and protective worry that came with helping someone reach for their dreams. "Got a minute? Derek has a business proposition that might interest you."

As Anthone emerged from the kitchen, wiping his hands on his apron, he looked curious about the unexpected opportunity.

"Derek," I said as the two men started talking about catering possibilities and creative menu development, "if you ever want to talk about what happened during the investigation, or if you need anything at all..."

"I know," he said, his smile genuine and filled with gratitude. "Thank you, Eliza. For everything you and your friends did to clear my name and find the truth."

26

After Derek and Anthone left together to discuss the potential partnership over coffee at a quieter location, the diner settled into its normal comfortable rhythm. Jacquie was experimenting with a new blue corn pancake recipe that smelled amazing. I loved her commitment to changing the menu on a regular basis.

"You know," Kashvi said, checking her watch, "I should get back to the bookstore after I've eaten. Mallory's handling the morning shift competently, but the new mystery novel shipment is supposed to arrive today, and Mrs. Patterson requested first access to anything with poison in the plot description."

"Isn't that timing a little inappropriate?" I asked.

"Not for Mrs. Patterson," Kashvi laughed. "She said experiencing real-life mystery made her appreciate fictional ones even more. She wants to compare our investigation techniques to what the protagonists do in novels."

As the lunch crowd began arriving with its usual mixture of regulars and newcomers, I reflected on how quickly life had returned to something resembling normal.

The drama and genuine danger of the past ten days felt almost surreal now, like something that had happened to different people in a different town.

Today, my biggest worry was filling the gaps in my schedule with Will and Anthone taking on new responsibilities. Cassidey could cover but she needed to focus on getting her GED. I'd put an ad in the paper tomorrow.

Life was already back to normal. Jet was leading hiking tours and nature education programs, Kashvi was organizing mystery novel displays and book club discussions, and Derek was rebuilding his catering business with renewed enthusiasm. The former gang kids were continuing their community service projects and developing peer mentorship programs. Even Alistair, despite his increasingly dramatic retelling of events, was back to running Dunes with his usual theatrical flair and boring but reliable food.

"Eliza," George said, finishing the enormous breakfast, "I have an important question for you."

Now what had I done wrong? "What's that?"

"Are you planning to continue investigating every murder that happens in Nueva Vida, or can I count on you to stick to the restaurant business from now on and leave law enforcement to the professionals?" He smiled, but I could tell the question was serious.

I considered my answer, weighing my need to help people against his need to keep me safe. Was I serious when I said I was retiring? I went for teasing like he's tried. "Well, that depends on your department's performance. Are you planning to keep having unsolved murders in Nueva Vida?"

"God, I sincerely hope not," George said. "I'd like to go back to dealing with occasional drunk drivers, noise complaints, and the occasional permit violation. Normal small-town law enforcement problems."

"Then I think we have a mutually beneficial deal," I said. "I'll stick to feeding people and managing restaurant crises, and you stick to catching actual criminals through proper legal procedures."

"Deal," George said, standing up and leaving money on the counter. "Though I have to admit, you and your friends are good at this investigative work. If any of you ever want to consider a career change to law enforcement..."

"Not a chance," I said. "I like my mysteries fictional, my crimes solved by professionals, and my life as peaceful as possible."

As George headed for the door, he paused and looked back with an expression I couldn't quite read. "Eliza, would you be interested in having dinner again sometime soon? Somewhere that doesn't involve murder investigations, corruption scandals, or official police business?"

I felt my cheeks warm and reminded my hormones I needed to stop playing the field at some point. "I'd like that very much."

"Excellent. I'll call you later today to set something up." His smile was genuine. "You know, Nueva Vida is lucky to have you and your friends. This community is stronger and safer because you care enough to fight for what's right, even when it's dangerous."

After he left, I stood behind the counter watching the familiar rhythm of lunch service begin—the comfortable chaos of orders being called, food being prepared, and conversations flowing over shared meals. The afternoon crowd had grown into a reliable stream of construction workers grabbing quick sandwiches, office workers escaping for proper meals, families with children who were enthusiastically debating what constituted acceptable lunch choices. EB EATS was definitely part of the community now.

"Another successful case for the EB Eats Investigation Society," Jet said with a grin.

"Don't even think about making that official," I warned with mock severity. "The last thing this town needs is anything that might encourage us to seek out more mysteries."

"Oh, I was looking forward to ordering business cards," Kashvi said with exaggerated disappointment as she looked for her wallet. "EB Eats Investigation Society: We solve mysteries and serve excellent coffee. Reasonable rates for amateur detective work. But I guess your boyfriend doesn't need the competition."

I threw a clean dish towel at her, but I was laughing with the relief that comes after surviving something terrifying. Sometimes the very best part of solving a mystery was getting back to the ordinary magic of friendship, community connections, and the simple pleasure of serving good food to people you cared about. "He's not my boyfriend."

"Not your only one," Jet said as he pulled the check from Kashvi and paid.

"A girl needs some fun," I said. I didn't need to choose, right? Or if I did, it was for another day.

WANT MORE

When an important food critic comes to Nueva Vida, every chef in town wants to impress. What happens when a body turns up?
Use the QR code below to buy your copy now!

REVIEW

If you enjoyed reading With a Side of Death, please consider helping other readers to find the story by using the QR code to leave a review.

FREE BOOK

Claim your copy of Burned by BLT when you sign up for my newsletter learn how Eliza became so determined to clear her name. Use the QR code below to get your free copy.

ALSO BY POPPY

For more books by Poppy Bridgeman

scan the QR code below.

ABOUT POPPY BRIDGEMAN

Hi, I'm Poppy Bridgeman, the cozy mystery alter ego of Canadian author P A Wilson. Poppy was "born" because sometimes stories need a gentler touch—with a little magic, a dash of humor, and plenty of sleuthing spirit.

As Poppy, I write the *Witch of Henbane Island* series (where witches and festivals collide with mysteries), the *EB Eats Culinary Mysteries* (a small-town diner, a determined heroine, and murder on the menu), and the *Pages & Paws Bookstore Mysteries* (a Devon bookshop, two mischievous corgis, and plenty of secrets tucked between the shelves).

When I'm not tangled in my characters' escapades, I'm happily tangled in yarn—I knit, weave, and doodle in sketchbooks between writing sessions. I also love to travel, finding inspiration for charming settings, quirky characters, and suspicious strangers wherever I go.

Home base is the Vancouver area, where I juggle writing as both Poppy and P A Wilson. Whichever name is on the cover, I'm always chasing the next story.

ACKNOWLEDGMENTS

People think that the process of writing is solitary. That's not the case for me. I have help from so many people it would be hard to acknowledge everyone, but I'll give it a try.

The support and inspiration I get from my writer's groups is incalculable. The Vancouver Writers Social Group opens my mind to other ways of telling a story. The Royal City Literary Arts Society gives me the opportunity to meet and share with other writers who have more knowledge than I do. The Other 11 Months group is where I learn about getting the words on the page. And my critique group who helps me find the best parts of the story I want to tell. Thanks to all of the members of these great groups.

Last of all, but definitely a huge part of the process, my beta readers. These are the people who love stories and are willing, and more than able, to tell me if my finished story is ready for you, my readers.